FROZEN FLOWERS FALLEN

BELLA AND THE BEAST MASTER

SARAH WESTILL

A GEN-HEIRS WORLD NOVELLA

FROZEN FLOWERS FALLEN

Bella and the Beast Master – Book 1

Copyright 2022 by Sarah Westill

ISBN 978-1-955293-15-0

Cover Design by For the Muse Designs

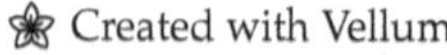 Created with Vellum

OTHER TITLES BY SARAH WESTILL

GEN-HEIRS: The Guardians of Sziveria (in reading order)

Levkaseon – A Prequel

Wintersfall

Raiventon

Kynhaven

Asherwick

Ericksen - A Wintervail Special

Survaine (April 27, 2023)

Bella and the Beast Master

Gen-Heirs world series

Frozen Flowers Fallen

Perfect Melody Silenced (February 6, 2023)

For world maps be sure to visit www. sarahwestill.com

To get the latest updates, follow Sarah on Instagram

@authorsarahwestill

Dedication and Acknowledgement

For Joseph, who thinks my created world is the most amazing thing ever and is always willing to help me imagine what a post-cataclysmic world would be like…

CONTENT WARNING:
This book contains mature content
Reader discretion is advised.

1

Sziverian National Investigative Division
  Haven City, Sziveria
  801 P.C.E. (Post-Cataclysmic Event)

THEY SUSPECTED THE WRONG MAN.

Bella Fenwick set the file she'd been carrying on the edge of the table, careful to remain unnoticed. No one ever paid attention to her, and if they did, she wasn't doing her job right. Serving as clerk to the lead investigative guardian under the Serial Crimes Unit for the Sziverian National Investigative Division meant she had to be a shadow. Unobtrusive. Since she'd landed the job by sheer luck three years ago, she worked hard not to do anything to jeopardize her position.

Guardians Reyes Avner and Marion Hinke stood around a glass topped table, peering at evidence illuminated from above. Both leaders of an investigative team, they'd been paired to-gether to solve a serial murder case that had taken a critical turn. Another female assistant took notes as they spoke. The words weren't conversational. More to convince the two who talked that they were right, correct in their as-sumptions of guilt concerning the man they'd pegged for the long string of homicides. Bella gritted her teeth to keep silent and pushed the folder closer to the collection of evidence. The feeling in the pit of her stomach wouldn't allow her to walk away. Deep inside, she *knew* they'd overlooked crucial pieces to a very large puzzle.

"When is the savage due to arrive?" Marion asked, tapping her pen along the edge of the table.

"He's not a savage," Reyes replied.

Marion waved a hand, annoyance scrunching her face. "All Ruthenians are sav-ages. Cold land, cold hearts."

Reyes shoved his hands into his pockets and leaned further over the table. Bella held her breath. "Spent a lot of time there, have you?"

"I was sent up there for a month a couple summers ago, cross-cultural training they'd called it." Marion shook her head. "Useless en-deavor. Ruthenians don't care about any culture but their own."

Reyes offered a noncommittal sound. His gaze flickered briefly to the folder and Bella squeezed her fists so tight her nails bit into her palms. *Look at it!*

"You'll see," Marion said, lifting her chin into the air.

"Perhaps. As for when we're supposed to meet the liaison, at some point today is my understanding, which is why I wanted us to go over this evidence once more. If he can be present when we level the accusations and receive a certificate of custody for the suspect, he can return home on the next ship bound for Ruthenia. Tie this up before we even have to worry about his helping in the investigation."

Bella wanted to ask what would happen with relations between Sziveria and Ruthenia when the killer struck again, because they were going to accuse the wrong man. She licked her lips and swallowed the question. Not her place. Not her job. She'd already interfered, anything more and she could wave her position goodbye.

Reyes glanced at the file again. The light from above glinted off his dark brown hair, styled in a short, neat cut off his ears and neck, long enough on top to be swept from his forehead. He angled his torso toward file, pulling the shoulders of his shirt tight. Marion stared. Bella was used to the effects of the handsome guardian. At one time she'd appreciated his masculine charm, maybe a little too much.

Guardian Reyes Avner was the kind of catch every woman in Sziveria hoped to achieve. Women like Bella couldn't hope for men like him, though. His future would eventually lead to a ranked guardianship, either through the

SNID or marriage. Entering a marriage contract with someone like her would be the equivalent of social suicide. She could offer nothing beneficial. No hope of genetically talented children. No hope of a ranked guardianship within her family lines. Reyes was nice to look at, but useless to dream about. No point in pining for the impossible.

"What's this?" he asked, pulling Bella from her musings. "Did I leave something on my desk?"

Bella cleared her throat. "No, Guardian Avner. I, um," she licked her lips and cleared her throat again, "I thought you should be aware of more evidence, is all."

"*You* thought?" Marion asked, her tone and raised brow conveying her disgust at Bella's meddling. "My dear girl, if we wanted the opinions of administrators, we'd ask. You can't possibly know the difference between all the cases you file for Guardian Avner. All you're doing is hindering our work. You've worked here long enough to know better."

"Bella has shown remarkable insight on cases in the past," Reyes conceded, sliding the file closer, his gaze on her face. Disapproval turned his mouth down and Bella's heart jumped into her throat. "However, always with my input."

The chance to convince them that what she'd found had value, merit, needed to be reviewed, was slipping away fast. Bella took a step closer. "I've learned a lot under you, and I really think that—"

Marion snatched the folder from Reyes's hand and tossed it to the opposite side of the table. "Leave the investigating to the guardians."

The urge to defend the findings burned in Bella's chest. She inhaled to speak, only before she could utter a single word, a young man burst into the room, straightening his hat that nearly flopped off his head in his rush.

"Guardians," he said, inclining his head to them both, "Beast Master Markus Ralston has arrived and is almost here. I thought you'd want to know."

Marion's jaw clenched and she cast Bella an angry glare. "Look what you've done! Wasted our time, and for what? For a little attention?"

Bella snapped her head back as if she'd been physically slapped. "N-no, I just—"

Marion waved a hand. "I don't care. Leave us."

Reyes frowned and stuffed his hands back into his pockets. "If I need anything, Miss Fenwick, I'll send for you."

Bella bowed her head in acknowledgement. "Very well, Guardian Avner."

Failure sat like a stone in her stomach. Bella pressed a hand to her belly and grimaced as she left the room. What else could she do? So many if only's filtered through her mind. If only she'd been born a Gen-Heir with a genetically inherited gift that mattered, could make a difference, then perhaps they would have listened to her. If only she knew the right words to say to be taken seriously. If only she weren't a weak introvert with pathetic social skills… If only she knew how to make sure the killer wouldn't strike again by finding the right man instead of the wrong one. She was none of those, and because of that, another woman would die.

THE URGE TO LAUGH MANIACALLY ALMOST BECAME more than Markus Ralston could bear. The stares. Oh, the stares. And the gasps from the women, and the cowering of the men as he and his female Ruthenarc wolf walked by was too much.

I want to snarl, I want, Lunah said along their bond, her humor vibrating within him along with her words.

I do not think I could bear their reaction without laughing.

No dignity, they have no dignity. Cowards. How have they survived, how?

We are guests, Lunah. Behave.

She gave a low chuffle of disapproval, but remained relaxed at his side. Markus ruffled the black-tipped silver hair between her ears, an easy task since her head reached his hip. Her pink tongue lolled out of her mouth and Markus shook his head. His beautiful wolf couldn't look less threatening. And yet the fear in the room became so thick he could smell it through their bond. She sneezed, licked her muzzle, and let her tongue once again flop out of her mouth.

The room he'd been told to meet the guardians in came into view. The door stood open, yet empty. So far Sziveria had not impressed him. No one had greeted him upon his arrival at Port Scarbrough. He'd gone through import and immigration just like every other visitor. No one had bothered to receive him at their official building. If he hadn't believed the country was merely appeasing his elected ruler before, he would now.

High Marshal Zan Veska had made a personal request of Markus. An honor to be asked by his ruler, and a favor now owed should Markus ever require one. Saying no wasn't an option. So here he was, an imposing presence in a country that'd rather ignore than help him. Fine. At thirty-two he was too old to play silly games and have hurt feelings. In Ruthenia, his talent and former rank as a ground commander for the Ruthenian Guard, awarded him enough respect. He didn't need the same from foreigners.

Lunah waited for him to enter the room first. Only a single light shining onto a large, round glass table illuminated the windowless room. A man and woman stood over a collection of objects and paperwork, muttering between themselves, while another woman stood in the shadows, scribbling on a pad of paper.

"Lunah, *Osat'yi*," Markus commanded aloud instead of through their bond, asking her to stay. She ambled over to a spot along the back wall and lay down in an elegant folding of her long, powerful limbs. The room went quiet and still. Markus returned his attention to the two at the table, a brow raised in question. "The guardians I'm to work with, I presume?"

The man recovered first, coming from around the table with an extended hand. "Guardian Reyes Avner, I'm a lead investigator for one of the five Serial Crime Unit teams."

The woman opted to remain at the table. She raised a hand in greeting. "Guardian Marion Hinke, also a lead investigator."

"Markus Ralston." He gestured to his wolf. "Lunah."

They want me to be invisible, they want, she huffed through his mind.

"Lovely," Marion said, an attempted smile twisting her face into more of a grimace.

"Thank you," Markus replied, his smile all teeth. Marion blinked and took a step back.

"Right, well, shall we?" Reyes motioned to the table. "We have all the evidence laid out for your inspection. We already believe we know who the suspect is. We're waiting on a certificate of custody now so we can level the accusations. Once we do, we'll bring him to the nearest

Haven City Enforcement Services building to be imprisoned until his hearing."

"You managed all this in the last week?" Markus asked, joining them at the table. He picked up a clear vial containing a petal-less flower stem.

"When we learned the identity of the latest victim was the daughter of a Ruthenian Provincial Marshall, we put all our resources into the investigation. We want to catch this guy as much as you do," Reyes answered.

Markus set the vial down next to seven others, and slid a glass box closer. A copper necklace lay inside, the chain broken. Another glass case contained a silver promise band, sprinkled with flecks of dried blood. He frowned. "I thought all the victims were strangled?"

"They were," Marion said. "But some fought back. We believe the blood on the bracelet is from the murderer. We expect him to have defensive wounds."

"From my understanding," he said slowly, pushing the evidence boxes back to the center of the table, "the killer has been around for five or six years, yes?"

"We suspected a serial killer situation two years ago for murders that have been happening since 794, correct," Marion replied, her pen flicking an annoying *tap-tap-tap* against the edge of the table.

"And you believe you found him in a week?"

"Not just a week. We've been investigating for those two years," Reyes said.

Doubt filled Markus. The case was too neat. Solved too quick. They wanted to wrap the little problem of a national incident up with a glittery bow and receive a pat on their heads for a job well done. A folder off by itself caught his attention and he slid it closer. He flipped open the file. Pages and pages of catalogued evidence, witness testimony, autopsies, and scene sketches filled the dossier, including of Mina Endler, Provincial Marshall August Endler's daughter. Markus stopped and looked over the scene sketches. All he had were the radio transmissions and personal assurances from the Arch Guardian Vestevno, who oversaw all the divisions of the SNID, that the killer would be found. Actual evidence piqued his curiosity.

"Is this a full compilation of all the murders?" Markus asked, turning a page to another scene sketch.

Marion gasped and tried to take the folder, but Markus slammed his hand down. "That was just something a clerk brought to us and doesn't pertain to this case."

"No?"

Marion's cheeks flushed red. "No. Everything you need is right here. I'll answer any questions you have."

Through his connection to Lunah, he knew Marion spoke the truth as she perceived it. His wolf could scent a lie. Markus looked over the collection of stacked glass boxes, and neatly arranged vials. More was missing than revealed. He closed the folder and tucked it under his arm. "I'm good, thank you. I'll find you again if I think of anything."

He left the room with their sputtering confusion behind him. Lunah joined him at his side and Markus held the folder down. *Lunah, Straes'ya*, he commanded.

Her nostrils flared and twitched over the file and then she lifted her nose into the air and sniffed again. *This way, she is this way.* Lunah trotted off through a collection of arranged desks forming a maze through the open floor.

She? Markus asked.

She, yes, she.

Lunah moved unimpeded through the crowded workspace, everyone stepping out of their way as they moved by. One man even leapt onto his desk with a yelp that had Markus wanting to snap his teeth and see if he could make the man reach the ceiling. The usual rumble of constant conversation was absent, replaced by a hushed murmur, whispers and shuffling paper. Every gaze averted when he glanced their direction. Lunah stopped at a cross-section of desks and lowered her nose to the floor. She turned in a half-circle, around again, and then went right.

The scent led her to desks lined up in front of a row of offices. Windows between the doors allowed light from the rooms to filter through, making the area a little less depressing than the rest of the floor, shrouded in shadow and lamp light. Only the important people must be allowed natural light.

A lone woman sat at a desk near the end of the line. File cabinets created a pseudo wall from the rest of the office, and an aisle. Little spider plants and ivy sat atop three of the tall cabinets, adding a burst of color. Chaotic, loose dark curls were gathered high atop her head into perhaps what had started as a bun this morning, but more hair had escaped than remained contained. The combination of muted natural light and the warm flame of lamps cast her pale brown skin in a golden glow. For a moment, Markus could do nothing except stare.

Not conventionally beautiful, her face was a little too round, her eyes a little too big for that, but all her features together were stunning. Full lips, a graceful jaw, small chin, a nose with a little tip and slightly flared nostrils, and delicately curved brows. The desk hid half her body, what remained visible was lean. Narrow shoulders, slender arms, and long fingers. The navy sweater she wore swallowed the rest of her torso, leaving him to imagine whatever curves were hidden from view. He wanted to do more than imagine. Wanted to know if her breasts would fill his palm or maybe just his mouth.

Lunah shook herself, pulling him from his reverie. The woman started, her palms pressing to the papers littering her desk. She blinked eyes a disconcerting shade of ocean green.

"H-hello," she said, tucking loose curls behind her ears. "Can I help you?"

Markus held up the file. "I'd like to know more about this."

2

———

BELLA IMAGINED IF HISTORICAL FIGURES, immortalized within paintings on museum walls, could peel themselves from canvas and march into the world, the man standing before her would be one of those individuals. She certainly could visualize him swinging a heavy iron hammer, saturated in blood and bellowing on a battlefield. A mythical Viking. He even wore a long fur lined leather coat, accentuating his tall, large frame. For the first time, Bella realized a man might be taller than her, rather than matching her height. An untrimmed beard hid the bottom half of an intense face. The light was too poor for her to know the shade of his dark hair, pulled tight from his forehead in a braid, the length hidden behind his back. Golden eyes stared at her, bright against his tan skin.

Her focus shifted from his face to his hand, holding up a file, down to the massive canine. The wolf-dog lay down, front paws extended, back legs relaxed to the side. Silver fur covered the wolfs torso and faded to a rich slate gray at the paws and muzzle. The thicker fur along the dog's shoulders and between the dark ears was tipped in black. A long, black fluffy tail swished in a lazy arc along the tile floor.

"Beautiful wolf," Bella said.

"Thank you," the man replied, coming behind the row of desks and grabbing the chair from the empty station next to hers. Silver flashed on his right hand, a thin ring on his pinky and wider one on his index finger. "Her name is Lunah. I'm Markus Ralston."

His words rolled with a pleasant, almost sharp accent. "The Ruthenian."

He inclined his head. "*Dak*, that is me."

Bella hesitated for a moment before offering her hand. "I'm Bella Fenwick. I'm the clerk for Guardian Avner."

He sat before accepting her gesture. His fingers were dry and warm against hers. A thrill raced along her arm as his palm slid into place with a gentle squeeze. Too soon he released his grip and she glanced back at Lunah to keep him from seeing her displeasure. Her fingers curled in an attempt to capture the sensation of his touch.

"I don't think a mere clerk could see what you have seen," he said softly, placing the folder on the desk in front of her.

Panic clutched at Bella's chest, chasing away the odd effect of his touch. He was an important dignitary, a guest of her nation, and she was a nobody meddling in affairs well outside of her expertise. If Reyes found out... "I don't think anything," she said, licking her suddenly dry lips.

His gaze focused on her mouth, and he leaned forward then snapped back as though something had tugged him from behind. His unique golden eyes met hers and he blinked, shook his head, and glanced at Lunah. The wolf had shifted. Not a muscle twitched underneath her thick fur. Her ears were alert, her eyes staring with freaky intensity at Bella.

"What is going on?" Bella whispered, goosebumps rising along her skin.

Markus shook his head and rolled his shoulders. A gentle movement of air brought the scent of leather, rain-soaked forest, and man. Bella took a deep breath, filling her nose and lungs, her eyes fluttering closed. The second she realized her reaction, she pulled out of the odd state she seemed put in by this stranger.

"Nothing," he said, his voice deeper, gruff. Lunah whined and his jaw clenched. "I said it's nothing."

Bella opened her mouth to say she hadn't replied when she realized he hadn't been speaking to her. She lifted a hand toward the dog. "You talk to her?"

"Normally where others can't hear, but she wasn't listening that way," he grumbled.

Lunah gave a low, soft *woof*. Markus

scrunched his nose and made the *I-am-in-charge* face. An expression familiar to Bella thanks to her mother, who despite Bella's recent twenty-third birthday, demanded consistent parental respect with *the look*. Drawing on willpower, Bella didn't burst into laughter at the peculiar exchange between canine and man. She used the distraction to slide the research folder to the opposite side of her desk, where she could then nudge it into the drawer and out of view. No one ever had to know, or acknowledge, her mistake again.

"I'm afraid I don't know much about your Gen-Heir talent," she said.

He looked at her again. Being his sole focus made her feel somehow prey to his predator. She had the urge to sit very still. "Gen-Heir? What is this?"

"Oh, right, sorry. A Genetic Heir, you know," she motioned from him to Lunah, "your beast master ability. Your mother or father had it, correct?"

"Everyone in Ruthenia has a genetic inheritance. Our society was born from the first generation to have special gifts," he said. "We don't have a name for what we all are, just Ruthenians."

Bella had heard the legends about the Ruthenians being the primary, and for hundreds of years, the only civilization to have genetically inherited talents. Then, when the dust of a world gone crazy after an apocalyptic event that reshaped the known world had settled, some had explored. They'd brought their strong genetic traits with them, and generations later, as new societies developed and blossomed, those traits made themselves known.

Sziveria referred to those born with inherited talents as Gen-Heirs, and placed great value on some of the more useful gifts. Bella's mother was a Gen-Heir, but without practical application to the government. Madeleine Fenwick made love matches with unerring accuracy, *if* the couple listened. Not all matches were meant to be. Bella's father had been gen-common, and as far as anyone knew, all his children were gen-common, too. Being able to work in a government job without a Gen-Heir ability was nearly unheard of. Bella had tested high enough to qualify for a clerk's position in academia. Those around her never wasted an opportunity to remind her how thankful she should be for the opportunity. She couldn't imagine growing up in a society like the one he explained, where everyone was equal.

He leaned forward, resting his elbows on his knees. The front of his loose shirt gaped open, revealing a muscular chest with a dusting of hair. Bella wondered what exploring all the textures would be like. Muscle, skin and hair… they all offered a tantalizing fantasy of sensation. She puzzled over the desire. Sure, she found men attractive. The one she worked for came to mind. But she'd never once been curious about what lingered beneath Reyes's clothes.

Never experienced a peculiar thrill by a mere touch.

"I will answer any questions you have," he said, "if you will answer mine."

"About?"

He lifted a finger. "The file."

Bella wiggled in her seat. "I'm not really involved with the cases like that. I only… file."

A dark brow crept up. Disbelief tightened his face. "File."

"Yes."

"Yet you put together a comprehensive collection of details from victims and cases."

She squirmed again. "Well, yes, but I have to read all the cases that come through to make sure they're properly filed."

His gaze narrowed. "And you saw something, but they wouldn't listen."

Breath caught in Bella's throat. "How did you…"

A small smile curved his mouth. He kept the mustache part of his beard neatly trimmed, framing sensual lips, with a fuller bottom than top. "They ignored me as well."

Bella stared at him in shock. "They *ignored* you?"

"They wouldn't talk to me about what you'd found."

"They don't know what I've found."

His hand grasped hers before she could react. Warm and calloused. Strong. The pad of his thumb slid along her palm, leaving behind tingles that traveled all through her body. "Tell me."

Bella meant to tell him no. Meant to deny the importance of her discovery. Something else came out instead. "All right." She looked at the row of file cases that provided the illusion of privacy. "But not here."

He stood and Lunah rose. "Where?"

Bella gathered the file and took a deep breath. "We'll go to my house."

THE CITY ROLLED BY THROUGH THE HORSE-DRAWN carriage window. Wet brick and stone glistened in the misty mid-afternoon. Pale gray clouds diffused the sun. A small, sleek vehicle zipped by and Markus pressed to the window to try to catch another glimpse of it.

"You've never seen an Ariot?" Bella asked.

Her sultry voice did things to him. Made him want to act like an idiot and roll on his back, show his belly. Be vulnerable. Somehow deserving of someone so young and vulnerable herself.

"No. It's too cold in Ruthenia. We only have two temperate months, not worth the expense of the magnetically powered engine and thin exterior. What is it made of, stretched canvas?"

Bella leaned close to peer out the window with him. Her upswept curls brushed his cheek.

So close, her scent of sugary vanilla and berries surrounded him. Good enough to lick. Lunah chuffed from the floor. A reminder. His kind couldn't find a mate outside of Ruthenia. It wasn't done. Those who did were banished, their offspring unwelcome in a land that prided itself on genetic purity. Bella Fenwick was off limits. Forbidden from tasting. Touching. *Wanting*. All things he'd do in his mind and never able to act on.

At least he shouldn't.

He couldn't seem to stop himself from giving in to temptation when the opportunity presented itself to touch her. Her hand, fingers, wrist… little stolen moments.

"I think the cheaper ones are made of canvas, but others are made of very thin shaped metal," she answered. "Show of wealth, I suppose, to be able to drive around in a rare commodity."

"They look so odd," he murmured, feeling like a little boy seeing his first train again. A wonder of their world, once taken for granted by their ancestors centuries before.

"I've heard a rumor they're trying to make them big enough to seat two."

"Would you ride in one?"

She sat back, gnawing on her delectable bottom lip. He wondered if the lip gloss she wore had a flavor, like strawberries, that so many women enjoyed sweetening their mouths with. He wanted to find out.

We are not here for you to find a mate, we are not,

Lunah chastised in his mind. He glanced down to find her glaring at him, her amber eyes slits of displeasure.

I know what we are here for.

"I think it depends on who the driver would be," Bella finally answered, pulling Markus from his perturbed wolf.

The Ariot found an opening between carriages and edged away. Markus kept sight of it until the little vehicle disappeared. Sighing, he settled back into his seat. The view shifted from tall brick apartment and hotel buildings to neighborhoods of two-story brick or stone homes. Greenhouses rose above the back of each dwelling, like sentinels of sparkling glass set into skeletal frames. A familiar sight, since Ruthenians also relied on greenhouses year-round to have access to living plants and food.

Markus expected them to stop at one of the middle-class homes, but the carriage continued. The view changed from individual lots to single story wood framed and clapboard sided homes crammed close together. A few multi-level homes were scattered among the shacks, but they didn't look much nicer. Wood checkered window panes where glass had been shattered and not replaced. Boards hung from the sides of houses where nails had popped free and no one bothered to fix them. Stairs sagged. Waxed canvas covered ruined shingles. Chimneys and stove pipes belched thick black smoke from lack of cleaning. No greenhouses, though he noticed what appeared to be side porches made of glass walls, so perhaps window gardens.

The carriage rolled to a stop at a street corner. The driver pounded on the roof to let them know they'd arrived. Markus jumped out first, followed by Lunah. He helped Bella down, another excuse to feel her long, delicate fingers slide against his rough palm. He didn't want to let go when her feet touched brick. The hesitation didn't seem to be with him alone. Fingers threaded through his, Bella stood on the sidewalk, her gaze on their locked hands. The driver made a noise and she jumped, yanking her hand free. Markus scowled. Lunah snapped her teeth in reaction to his annoyance. Bella paid the driver, adjusted the leather satchel slung across her chest, and motioned for him to follow.

The wooden wheels and horses' hooves clacked on the brick as the carriage rolled away. Markus squinted through the falling mist, still frowning. "Why didn't he drive us to your home?"

Bella wrapped a hand around the thick leather strap of her satchel. "Drivers don't like The Rows. The streets are narrow and it's easy to fall prey to thieves. They'll go as far as Beekman Avenue here, and drop off at the start of any row that meets up with the avenue, but not into The Rows themselves."

A brisk wind picked up greasy wrappers, discarded paper, and dead leaves, swirling and tossing the bits of trash around. A small glass jar rolled and bounced along the sidewalk before settling in a thick crack. The putrid scent of rot and burning wood mixed with the food cart set up across the street. Markus wrinkled his nose, while Lunah lowered her head and pawed at her muzzle.

"You live here?" Markus asked.

Her chin lifted into the air. Defiance brightened her already vivid ocean green eyes. "Yes."

A broken gate flapped and banged against a fence, its hinges squeaking in protest. Markus followed behind Bella, alert. Lunah kept close to his side, her fur brushing his thigh with each step. The road between the houses was indeed narrow, more suited to bicycle travel or a horse and rider than a cart or carriage. Curtains fluttered in windows from watchful neighbors. Somewhere a cat yowled, joined by a deeper, more desperate wail. The yowling turned to outright feline screaming.

A woman called out crude words from a door, an invitation, for a price. "Why let the cats have all the fun, eh?" she cackled, hefting sagging breasts up with both hands.

Bella flinched and walked faster, giving him a lovely view. Tall and willowy, she wasn't what could be considered curvy. But as he watched her round butt move with each step, he fantasized about how firm and sweet she'd be filling his palms. Her hips were narrow, waist small. Markus tried to imagine her walking home alone, in the dark, night after night where hired drivers wouldn't even venture, and frowned. "Why does a clerk for the SNID live in such a dangerous part of the city?"

"This isn't that dangerous," she said, shoving her hands into her coat pockets. The jacket was short, and didn't quite fit together at the edges for her to button. "Old City Ruins is the worst part of the city. Not even Haven City Enforcement Services ventures into that part of town. Southern Row has its own division. The houses might look bad, but HCES takes care of the people here. We're safe. Well, as safe as an any inner city can be, I suppose."

They turned a corner and headed deeper into the destitute neighborhood. "You didn't answer the question. Does your government not pay their employees well?"

"Perhaps I didn't answer because it's not your concern," Bella said, a hard edge to her voice.

"Ah, something personal you don't want to talk about."

She cast a sharp glance over her shoulder. "Correct."

A mystery, then. He took in the sights around him once more. "If I figure out the reason, will you tell me if I'm right?"

She stopped and turned so fast he almost ran into her. "If you figure out why I'm living in The Rows instead of where? Where is someone like me supposed to live?"

"One of the apartment buildings closer to the

SNID. Or one of those homes with the large greenhouses off the back we passed by." He gestured to the house on the right. The corner posts were missing from the porch, making the overhang slump. Missing boards around the bottom opened the underside of the dwelling to vermin. Moss and sprouting trees grew from the rotting wood of the roof. "Not somewhere with a leaking roof, broken windows, and a fire hazard for heat."

A shadow flickered in her eyes and she turned away, motioning at the house. "My home is not this one."

"Still, if I ascertain the reason, will you tell me?"

She looked over her shoulder at him, her jaw working. "Why does it matter to you?"

Markus considered her question. "I'm not sure."

She blinked at him and returned her attention to in front of her. "Well, at least you're honest."

"Did you expect different?"

"I didn't expect anything. I don't know you."

"Yet you're taking me to your house." He caught up to her, forcing Lunah to walk either behind or ahead. She chose ahead.

"We won't be alone."

Markus hadn't thought to ask about a husband, or even a live-in lover, though he knew the latter was rare in Sziveria. Human Rabies Syndrome was still a very real threat, a sexually transmitted virus that turned its host into a literal zombie for a few hours before final death. Every nation had dealt with the lethal illness differently. Sziveria opted to allow the casual relationship to become safer, more stable, by couples entering into marriage contracts for a length of time of their choosing, with a minimum year. Most couples could manage to remain together for a year, the safety of their monogamous relationship protecting them from infection.

HRS hadn't affected Ruthenia like most nations, as Ruthenians mated for life via a bond other populations didn't experience. Their genetics allowed the bond, and between beast masters, it was even stronger. Another reminder of why he couldn't act on his attraction to the woman at his side. She'd never be able to bond with him the way he was meant to with a mate.

"Husband?" he asked, clasping his hands behind his back.

She snorted. "Mother."

The relief that rushed through him took him by surprise. "Still, you place a lot of trust in a stranger to bring me to your home. With my wolf."

She cast him a sideways glance. "You don't know my mother."

NERVOUSNESS RODE BELLA HARD AS SHE unlocked the front door of her ramshackle home. While granted, the house was better kept than its neighbors, there were still boards where the landlord refused to replace cracked or busted windowpanes. The once yellow paint, now more of a nasty shade of dirty cream, chipped and peeled off the clapboard, showing the aging wood underneath. Inside, however, the furniture was decent. The floors were clean.

Bella led him through the entry and front hall into the small living room that also tripled as their kitchen and dining room. Her mother stood at the cast iron stove, peeling shells off beans to soak in boiling water. A long braid of rich brown hair fell to her full hips. Not for the first time, Bella lamented she'd inherited her father's thin frame rather than her mother's curvaceous figure. Madeleine glanced over her shoulder, doing a double take the second she realized Bella hadn't arrived alone.

"Hey, Momma," Bella said, kissing her mother's unlined cheek in greeting. Even at forty-five, her mother maintained a youthful beauty, her only claim to age the soft wrinkles around her eyes and mouth. "This is Markus Ralston from Ruthenia and his wolf Lunah. He's working a serial case with the SNID." She gestured from Markus to her mother. "Markus, this is my mother, Madeleine Fenwick."

Madeleine wiped her hands on a small towel and then offered her fingers. Markus accepted with a brief shake, but Madeleine didn't let him go. She gripped his hand in both of hers and held tight, a huge grin on her pretty face. "You know."

Markus's gaze narrowed. They stared at each other for a long moment, making Bella squirm. Then he gave a curt nod and Madeleine released his hand. Bella looked between the two of them.

"Know what? What does he know?' When her mother remained silent, she looked at Markus. "What do you know?"

Bella might as well not have been in the room. Madeleine cast another smile at Markus, holding out her hand. "Can I take your coat?"

Markus shrugged out of the lengthy, heavy jacket. He handed Madeleine the garment and Bella stared at his broad shoulders and the thick braid falling midway down his back. A loose, long-sleeved dark cotton shirt covered his torso. Black canvas pants and leather boots helped him maintain the dangerous edge that losing the coat should have weakened. She thought perhaps he'd be smaller without the bulky outerwear, but he wasn't. He'd filled out the fur and leather all on his own.

He pushed up his sleeves to his elbows. A wide leather bracer enclosed his right wrist. In addition to the two rings on his right hand, a third ring glinted from his middle finger on his left. Bella had never seen a man wear anything more than a promise band and wedding ring. Jewelry for decoration on men wasn't common in Sziveria. On Markus, the objects were downright masculine, accenting his muscled forearm and long fingers. Sexy. Bella went to the stove to see what her mother had been cooking when they'd interrupted. Anything to change the focus of her errant thoughts.

Madeleine returned, a smile on her face. She knelt on the floor near Lunah. "May I?" she asked, glancing up at Markus.

Markus hooked his thumbs into his pants pockets and nodded. "Of course, she's very friendly."

"I have heard a rumor that beast masters prefer their animals not to be touched, something about them being a working animal," Madeleine said, holding her hand out to the massive wolf to smell.

"Giving her attention won't compromise her ability to work should she need to," Markus said. "Of course, some beast masters believe their animals are too important for simple affection. That it somehow makes them less... imposing."

As if to prove his point, Lunah rolled onto her back with a groan and wiggled, becoming the most nonthreatening beast Bella had ever seen. Her back legs flopped and her front paws curled into her chest. Madeleine scratched at her ribs, rewarded by Lunah's back leg twitching and a song of happiness from the canine. A ridiculous sliver of jealousy wiggled through Bella. Her mother was pleasing Markus's dog, when she hadn't even let the wolf smell her. Bella hadn't even thought to be introduced to the wolf beyond learning her name.

Bella looked up from the exchange to find Markus watching her. She unwound her satchel from body and laid it on the table. "You probably want to get started on the file so you can return to the SNID."

"Not really," he said softly. "You can touch her too, if you'd like."

Lunah flipped over and stared at Bella, muzzle twitching. Bella straightened her shoulders. "I don't know if she'd let me."

Madeleine stood after a quick pat between Lunah's ears. "I have to go to the market and get some sausage for the soup. I didn't know we'd have a guest for our meal tonight."

"Don't add anything extra on my account," Markus said.

Madeleine waved his words away. "Men like you need protein. More than beans and broth will provide."

"I can get it, Momma," Bella said, reaching for her satchel. "The bike is still at work. I don't want you to have to walk that far."

Madeleine untied the apron from around her waist and laid it on the only counter space between the stove and sink. "No, I know you have work to do. I'll be fine. Won't be the first time I've walked, no one bothers me." She gestured to the small round table with two seats. "Sit, do what you needed to do."

Markus looked at Lunah. She rose, stretched

her front paws, opened her jaws wide, shook her entire body, and then went to stand next to Madeleine. "Please allow her the honor of accompanying you."

Madeleine blinked down at Lunah. "I'm not sure what the store owner will say."

"She won't go in unless you want her to, and then what are they going to do?"

"I suppose you have a point." Madeleine chuckled, her focus on the wolf that reached to her waist. "Very well. Come on, pretty girl, let's take a walk."

Bella pulled a chair out and sat. Markus moved the seat across from her nearer, though she didn't know how he'd possibly fit so close to her at the small table. He managed, and she tried not to think about how good he smelled, or how the heat from his body made the fire burning unnecessary.

"The guardians at the SNID will notice we're both missing," she felt the need to point out.

"You were the one who suggested we leave." His deep voice washed over her. The heavy accent he spoke with, so different from hers, made him somehow more exciting. More dangerous. At least to her nerves, which seemed hyper alert in his presence.

"We couldn't stay. They'd have found us there well before they find us here."

"What makes you think they'll look for us here? We could have gone anywhere, including where I'm staying, with the Arch Guardian Wolvenguard."

Bella swallowed. "You're staying with an arch guardian?" Her words came out as more of a squeak than as anything intelligible.

"Well, yes. Who else would let me keep my wolf? He's a Sziverian born Ruthenian and was more than happy to let me use one of his many empty bedrooms."

Bella glanced around her tiny house again. An arch guardian, only answerable to the King or queen elect. Her miniscule living space became even more pathetic. "We should have gone there. No one would have dared knock on his door."

"I prefer your house." His gaze wandered the room, moving from the blanket draped couch, to the book covered end tables, the knit rug in the center of the room, to the wall that served as their kitchen. Small framed ink prints of nature graced the walls. "Feels like a home, not some outlandish need to impress. The arch guardian's mansion is all marble and polished wood. Impersonal, cold." He patted his thighs and then rubbed them with a content sigh. "Yes, I much prefer here."

At one time they'd had so much more. Beautiful paintings. Thick woven rugs from Syrinad that held stories in their patterns. A home that wasn't a hovel. If she thought about all they'd lost, she'd cry. And from experience she knew it'd be a long time before she could stop.

If her father had known this is where his choices would lead them after his death, would he have made different decisions? Forcing the melancholy thoughts away, she pulled her satchel close enough to flip open the buckle latch.

"They might not think to search for you here, you're right. I doubt they'd believe I'd be brave enough to bring you to The Rows. Not if you're staying with the arch guardian."

He smiled and her mind blanked. Sweet summer sun. Dimples. On both cheeks. They were equal parts cute *and* sexy, changing his entire appearance from intimidating to, if not approachable, simply human. She wanted to touch him. Wanted to know if the long fluff of his beard was coarse or soft. Wanted to know how warm his cheek would be under her caress. Found her fingers curled around the latch of her satchel to stop herself.

"Good thing they don't know anything about me," he said.

An effective reminder. She didn't know anything about him, either. Bella focused on the reason she'd brought a complete stranger to her home. Her country owed his an answer for a wrong committed on her land. She pulled the file free and set it in front of him.

"Did you know her? The victim?" she asked, folding her hands on the tabletop.

"No. I don't know her father, either. Not personally."

Bella pressed her lips together in thought. "Why did they send you, then?"

"Our high marshal asked me to come, and I *do* know him." He opened the file, removing pages and setting them in a neat stack in the center of the table.

Bella propped her elbow on the table, rested her chin on her palm, and regarded him. "High marshal, that's like our…"

"King or queen."

She didn't realize her mouth had fallen open until he nudged a knuckle under her chin and popped it closed. "You should be working with Master Guardian Perrella, not me. I-I'm nobody. A clerk. I file things."

"Your master guardian in charge of your division, your team leaders over units… none of them seemed to care. The only authority figure who's shown me any courtesy is Wolvenguard." Papers fluttered as he continued to sort. "You are not a nobody. So far, you're the only one who can help me."

"They won't let me," she said before she could stop. "This is all I can do for you."

He turned his head and stared at her. The shade of his eyes reminded her of fire. Deep, golden, intense. Heat blossomed across her cheeks and she fidgeted.

"You can do much more than you think. As for them *letting* you, I will worry about that." He motioned between the two of them. "You and me? We're handling this case together."

3

Bella wished she could gather Markus's confidence and wrap it around herself. She stared at him, eyes wide, no coherent words coming to mind. Pressing her palms to the cool wood of the table, she tried to center her thoughts.

"Mr. Ralston…"

"Markus."

Bella rubbed her hands down her face and took a deep breath. "Markus. I'm not an investigator. I know nothing about solving crimes."

"I do."

"Great," Bella said, wincing at the sarcasm she couldn't contain. She pressed her hands back onto the table. "If you know what you're doing, and you've been assigned a team already, what in the inhabited world do you need from me?"

"What I need," he took a sheet of paper and

gently set it before her, "is to know what you see when you look at this."

"A drawing," Bella stated deadpan.

He stared at her.

Bella gave a low growl of frustration in her throat. He matched the sound, deeper, stronger, much more convincing. She eased away from him and glared. "Fine, wolf man. I'll look. No need to go animal on me."

"You challenged first," he said.

She sighed. "Is that what I did? Forgive me, I'm not familiar with wolf etiquette."

He dipped his chin and leaned forward, his eyes so close to hers the irises looked like burning amber. "I think you are trying to distract from the task. Go on, Bella. Tell me what you see."

Bella dropped her hands into her lap and stared at the charcoal sketch, rendered by a crime scene artist. In academia, she'd read about fantastical, pre-cataclysm devices called cameras that had once allowed law enforcement to document crime scenes with unerring accuracy. Now, they had talented genetic heirs for such a task. Artists, who along with their ability to draw or paint, also had the namesake of such a marvel, a photographic memory. Technically, what Bella gazed upon held the same detail, captured by hand.

"What are you waiting for?" he whispered, his breath teasing the hair near her ear.

Bella resisted the urge to shiver. Wondered at

how a question could feel so intimate. "I'm not sure what you're expecting of me."

He set more scenes from the same crime in front of her, until the table was too covered for any more. "There is a lot of information in this file. Catalogued evidence. Witness statements. Autopsy results. But what you've included are all the crime scene sketches, even those some would consider trivial. Please," he urged again, sweeping a hand over the drawings. "Tell me what *you* see."

Nervousness fluttered in her stomach and dampened her palms. She rubbed her hands along her thighs. What he asked of her couldn't be done without touch. Doing so with sweaty hands that could ruin part of the image was unthinkable. She'd not destroy evidence needed to bring justice to the women. Would not spoil the chance to find their killer.

Squaring her shoulders, she rested her forearms on the edge of the table and tried to mentally prepare herself for an alternate reality she never could understand, but her mother had encouraged her since toddlerhood to accept. The first time Bella had touched a crayon scribbled picture of a stick tree forest and horse, and found herself lost in a world of pink trees and blue ponies, her mother had urged her to explore. To draw more. To get lost in her personal imagination land. Her artistic endeavors had never developed beyond the basic, but her odd ability had. Both her parents had held great hope for their youngest daughter, only for the expectation to be squashed at guardianship testing. There was no way to examine an unknown talent, and no way to convince anyone of its presence.

In the end Bella figured her odd ability was just that, inconsequential. Useless even. But if Markus wanted to know what she could *see*, then she'd tell him. Carefully, she rearranged the illustrations in the way that if she had been the scene artist, she would have meant for them to be viewed. As a whole, not individual. Bella cleared her mind. Let reality slip away as she brushed her fingers along the first image. By touch, she'd be able to enter the drawing, like a room she alone had the key for. In her mind, she opened her eyes. A world of black and white greeted her. Detailed lines of pencil created her new view. She stood in a room caught in a moment of time.

She looked around, her fingers sliding along the images as she turned in her mind, touching where she needed to scrutinize, the room building until she could walk around and inspect any detail she wished. The victim lay in shades of gray. Bella knew there were comprehensive drawings of the woman.

"Can you please place the sketches of the victim under my fingers," she asked.

Sensation fluttered under the pads of her fingers and she twitched, then knelt at the woman's legs. All the fine elements unfolded before Bella's sight. The little things that had bothered her.

"This victim was found a year ago," Bella said. "She is not considered part of the case you're investigating. Is that why you chose her?"

"Yes," Markus replied, his voice floating in the room around her. Odd to hear but not see him. Bella couldn't dwell on that, or allow her focus to waver. "I was curious why she mattered for my case. I believe there are three others."

"The killer likes to leave petals in the victims mouth. This woman had a whole bud, not just the petals. The other two had only petals, no part of the original stem. All three are a type of rose, whereas the others are varying flower types." Bella crouched near the woman's head. The urge to reach out and touch the intangible was strong. She'd touch whatever was in front of her in the real world, not here. "If the three victims alone were the murders they're seeking to blame their suspect for, perhaps they would have enough evidence for questioning. But they excluded these three from the case they're building against him. Therefore, the evidence they *do* have now is all wrong for who they're trying to accuse. Not that they had the right man to begin with."

"You sound very certain."

"I am, and it's frustrating. If I, a clerk, can see the gaping holes in their evidence, how can no one else?"

"Because they need to close this case or risk an international incident. No one wants that," Markus said.

Bella looked the woman over, frowning. "Why not show you what they have and accept your help, like you were sent here to do? Why lie?"

"I'm a foreigner, and to some, a barbarian, not good for much but hunting perhaps. Certainly not solving their crimes for them."

She tried to imagine anyone taking one look at Markus Ralston and seeing anything except intelligence. Danger? Of course. But on the sharp edge of his commanding personality, his intellect shone. Paper rustled, a flutter of noise with no reference. Bella rubbed her fingers along the drawings in front of her, maintaining contact to help keep herself in the illusion.

"Tell me why you think they have the wrong man?" he asked.

"Look at her," Bella said softly, staring at the woman, though drawn in death, still somehow peaceful, almost serene. "She must have been so scared when she died, and yet..."

"She's perfect. Not a hair out of place. Her clothing is as if she laid down to sleep in the middle of her floor," he reflected.

Bella smiled through sadness. "Yes. He took great care of her, didn't he? Some of his victims did fight back, and he didn't remove the evidence of their struggle from their fingernails, or even in one instance, her mouth. But in all the cases, he has fixed their hair, their clothes, their shoes. When they are found, violence is not the first thing that comes to mind."

"And the man they want to accuse of the crimes?"

Disgust unfurled in Bella's stomach and within her mind she stood. In slow steps she explored the victim's home as recorded. "He's a rapist, and as far as I know, which again might be limited, a very violent one."

"Never convicted?"

"No, the accusations never stuck. Not enough witnesses, the victims didn't do what they needed to preserve evidence, whatever the reason. He's been accused three times and walked free," she bit out. "He's mean, and while it's not hard to believe he'll progress to murder, when he does, it'll be unmistakable. Ugly and cruel. This," she waved a hand around the room, where she imagined when someone walked in, they *felt* the quiet, "is not a picture of brutality."

"Though the murders are still an act of violence."

"He strangles them, yes. With what, they don't know. Not his hands."

"And why do they believe this rapist is the answer?"

"He always sends his victims a single flower the next day."

"And all the women in this serial case have had single flowers left on their bodies in some form," he said.

A whisper of sound she couldn't place tugged her from the depths of the sketched crime scene. She blinked as her living room came into focus and turned to Markus. His fingers brushed through his beard, his gaze thoughtful. How interesting. Stroking his facial hair made noise. Once again, she found herself curling her fingers into her palm to keep from touching him.

"Is that their only link?" he asked. "The single flower?"

"Yes."

He scoffed and dropped his hand back to the file. "Weak. I never would have accepted their conclusion."

"They had all the evidence arranged to prove their case to you."

"Know what I think?" he asked, gathering together the scene laid out on the table.

Bella collected the papers closest to her. "What?"

"I think they assembled bits and pieces of cases that fit, found a suspect they needed off the streets to take the fall, and hoped I'd be too dumb to look beyond the surface."

Shocked, Bella paused halfway to a sheet and stared at him. "That's quite an accusation."

"What made you doubt?"

"I already told you."

"That was it? The flower?"

Bella looked away, uncomfortable.

"Guardian Avner would never risk his reputation by falsifying a case."

"And yet," he prompted, sweeping a hand over the file.

And yet she couldn't deny the awful truth in his observation. "What are you going to do?"

He shrugged. "What is there to do? Their word against mine? Useless. I already told you, we're going to figure out this case. You've done the hardest part, now catch me up. Lay it out for me, Bella."

"You want *me* to give you the case details?" she asked, pointing at her chest in disbelief.

"I doubt the investigators know half what you do. You organize, file, sort, and compile everything for your guardian boss, yes?"

"Well, yes, that's my job, but—"

He shook his head and held up a hand, halting her argument. "Please tell me everything you know." He slid the file closer to her. "From the very first documented murder to Mina Endler."

"I think it's best if I show you," she said, rising. She gathered the rest of the paperwork he'd laid out and then went through the folder, removing only the full body scene sketch of the victims. With all eleven images, she moved to their small living space. "There isn't enough room on the table."

He followed, a looming presence at her back. In rows of two, she laid the pages out across the long couch. When she finished, she stood back and let him review the remarkable discovery she'd made by accident.

"Incredible," he murmured, walking the length of the piece of furniture. "They're all lying exactly the same."

"Yes."

"What about physical features?"

All the images were black and white, making a quick study for additional resemblances difficult. "He doesn't seem to care about those. Hair, eyes, skin, height, weight, none of them arc similar enough to believe he has a type."

"Just gender."

"Yes. Social class also doesn't seem to matter. All the women are single, however, living alone."

"He'd have to learn that about them." He paced back to the other side of the couch, picking up an image, returning it to the lineup, and repeating the process with another. "Ages?"

"Between eighteen and thirty."

Markus took a step back, arms crossed, and stared down at the eleven women. "What do you think about the bud in the mouth instead of the petals?"

"I think he succeeded in his attempt once, and failed at the rest, but he'd already stuffed the thing in their mouth when it fell apart."

"Then he leaves the single, naked stem in their hands, resting on their chest."

She nodded. "Correct."

"Always in the center of the room." His jaw

flexed as he continued to look over the pictures from a short distance. "How were they discovered?"

Bella returned to the table and sat. She went through the folder and gave him the information he requested. "They were all found within twenty-four hours of death, either by a neighbor, friend, or an anonymous tip, from a police radio."

He stepped nearer to the couch and picked up a drawing. "A police radio?"

"Yes. Most of our cities have call boxes every few blocks for emergencies. They're tuned to the nearest Enforcement Services division."

"And all the calls from the anonymous tip were around the twenty-four-hour mark?"

She read over the information and nodded. "According to the reports, yes."

"That was the killer. So," he began, picking up another drawing, holding them side by side, "he wants them found within a twenty-four-hour window. Definitely fits what you said about them needing to be presentable. He has a compulsion for them to be found before death erases their beauty, and therefore his hard work."

Bella absorbed his casual statement. *That was the killer.* Spoken without a pause or a doubt. "The killer reported his own crime?"

"It's not uncommon. Did anyone make a note or pose the question in the file about it possibly being him?"

"Um..." She couldn't get past the revelation. What sort of man was so confident in his evil deeds that he walked without fear of being caught? To such an extent that he revealed his crime to the authorities? "Someone would have seen him at the call box. Someone would have noticed."

"No one interviewed about the radio on those occurrences?"

She sifted through the documentation. "I-I don't know. I didn't even think it to be relevant. Maybe those interviews are stored in evidence still, or my file cabinet."

He set the pages back down. The muscles in his shoulders and arms bunched and slid underneath the dark fabric of his shirt, catching the highlights from the fire. Bella shifted her focus back to the case folder. He angled toward the couch so his back was to her. The thick length of his braid swayed. Giving up hope on concentration, Bella surrendered to ogling him. Intricate plaited layers started at the crown of his head and ended below his shoulders. She stared, noting the play of light across the strands whenever he moved. His hair wasn't black, or even brown, but an unusual shade of deep wine red. Intriguing and unique, like the rest of him.

"Then that's where we'll start," he said, gathering all the images together in the order she'd laid them out. "When your *makyshka* returns with Lunah, we'll go back to the SNID and see if we can find the interviews from those dates. All the interviews, no matter how insignificant they might seem."

Uneasiness squirmed through her. "They won't let me work with you. I'm not qualified, nor is that my job position. If they reported back to your country that you've teamed up with a clerk…" She shook her head and gritted her teeth. "I can't imagine the insult your high marshal would take."

He handed her the stack of drawings. "I told you I'd take care of working with you. Trust me, I'll handle it."

THE CARRIAGE BOUNCED ALONG THE BRICK ROAD. The faint clomp of horse hooves and clatter of wheels helped ease the silence inside. Across from Markus, Bella shifted in the seat. Again. Sitting still hadn't been something she'd managed since he'd closed the door and the driver took off. She licked her tempting lips, leaving them glossy and plumped. Anxiety filled the space between them. Lunah whined at his feet, her ears and tail twitching.

Markus settled into the seat, spreading his arms wide and resting his bent elbows on the back. "You need to relax. Your stress is worrying Lunah."

Bella cast a glance down at Lunah, and an emotion he couldn't place tightened her mouth and jaw. "She doesn't care about me."

Lunah huffed in his mind. *I don't know her, I don't.*

Do you want to know her? he asked, brushing the toe of his boot along her furry leg.

It is not necessary, it is not.

For some reason, the answer rubbed him wrong. A sudden need for Bella to know his wolf bloomed in his chest. He straightened from the seat and held his hand out. "Let me see your hand," he said softly.

Wariness filled her gaze. "Why?"

Instead of answering, he motioned with his fingers for her to obey. She sighed and rested her hand on his palm. The instant awareness she brought made him want to pull her across the space. He wondered how different her kiss would be from others he'd experienced, if her touch alone kicked his heart into an excited rhythm. Her much smaller, narrower fingers trembled in his grasp.

Lunah rested on the floor between them, a hulking mass of muscle and fur. The gentle rocking of the vehicle made staying steady a challenge. He braced his feet further apart as he eased Bella's hand to Lunah. His wolf's nose twitched and flared. Her thick, rough pink tongue licked at the back of his hand. Markus covered Bella's hand with his and guided her fingers to between Lunah's soft, fuzzy ears.

Nice, she smells nice, Lunah said, her words holding a surprised edge.

Markus agreed. Sitting so close to her at her

dining room table, he'd been surrounded by her scent. By the sugary sweetness of her. When she'd been lost in the depths of her surprising genetic gift, he'd had to resist burying his nose in the crook of her neck. From tasting her soft skin. Lunah had no such polite restrictions. Her tongue lapped out and caught Bella on the inside of her forearm. A faint squeal hiccupped from Bella, then she laughed, her fingers burying deeper into Lunah's fur.

Her smile changed everything. A brightness illuminated her eyes and lit up her face, moving her from pretty to stunning. Her teeth were straight, and white, her front incisors slightly longer than the rest. Something new unfurled in his chest. Something… vivid. He rubbed at his sternum, not understanding the sensation.

"She is so beautiful," Bella murmured in wonder. "How long will she live?"

"Ruthenarc wolves bond for life. She could live as long as I do."

Bella's eyes widened. "Wow, I had no idea."

Markus shrugged. "Some beast master jobs are more dangerous than others, and the life expectancy of either wolf or man can be short."

"But if you are safe, then you both can live into old age together?"

"Yes."

She patted Lunah's head. "That's amazing, and special."

Markus massaged his fingers into the thick

hair at Lunah's neck. "Yes, she certainly believes she's something special."

Lunah turned her head and nipped at him. Markus snatched his hand away. Her teeth snapped at air. He laughed and touched two fingers to the top of her nose. *Still faster than you.*

I will get you some day, I will, she quipped, her tail slashing across his shin.

Bella sat back, folding her hands on her lap. "Is your talent uncommon in Ruthenia?"

"Not so much a wolf, no. Other animals are much rarer. There are enough of us born to bond with wolves to keep the breeders in business." Lunah shifted until her chin rested on the seat next to his thigh. Markus obliged her unspoken request and gently petted between her ears. "What about your talent?"

She blinked. "Mine?"

"Yes."

A flush deepened the light brown of her cheeks. "Being able to envision oneself inside a painting or drawing isn't exactly a useful gift."

"Is that what you can do?" he asked, unable to hide his astonishment.

She fidgeted and licked her lips again. "Yes."

His fingers curled into Lunah's fur as he sat forward. "Explain it to me."

Shrugging, she picked at a loose string around one of the upholstery buttons near her thigh. "Not much to explain. I touch an image and I'm *there*. The more angles, the more complete my surroundings. If there's enough, it's like I'm standing in a drawn or painted room, or forest, or even underwater."

"You can visit the scene of a crime over and over again?"

"Yes."

"Incredible."

She shook her head and let out a faint chuckle. "No, it's..." Pressing her eyes closed, she shook her head again. "It's a silly talent."

"You really believe that?" The exasperation on her face answered for her. Markus *tsked* and looked out at the city ambling past the window. "Your society has failed you if you truly think you have no value. Even without your talent, you *see*, Bella Fenwick."

"What does that mean?" she asked, confusion lacing her words.

"You see things others do not. Perhaps a fragment of your gift, perhaps just a talent all on its own, whatever it might be, you see things in a scene no one else does."

Her hand gripped the satchel slung across her chest, where the thick file rested. "I'm a clerk."

"Do you think if you say it enough, you'll believe it?" he asked, clenching his jaw.

Her nostrils flared and her grip tightened on the bag. "I need this job, Mr. Ralston. Please don't do anything to jeopardize my career. I will help as much as I can, but don't expect much."

Markus knew she didn't trust him. Nothing

had happened to give her the opportunity, or him the means, to earn the right. He'd walked into her life only hours ago and she didn't know him from any other stranger. Still, he chafed at her lack of confidence. In herself. In him. Stunned that he found himself caring one way or another.

"I guess I will have to teach you some things about yourself," he said.

She cast him a skeptical glare, but had no time to reply as they arrived at the SNID building, eight stories of gray stone and hulking shadows. One thing Sziveria had always seemed to lack was architectural imagination. All their government buildings bordered on depressing. The SNID building wasn't any different. Windows set out from the exterior, providing those lucky enough to get a windowed office the means to grow something green in their workspace. At the top, a roof greenhouse glittered in the mid-afternoon sun. Hard angles made up the four corners of the building. A deeply recessed front entry never saw any of the sun's rays trying to cut through the surrounding structures, leaving it cold regardless of the time of year.

Markus jumped out of the carriage first and helped Bella. He didn't want to let go of her hand once she was on the sidewalk. Lunah followed, leaping from the carriage and to Markus's side in one graceful move. Bella slipped her fingers free after casting him an odd look. He followed her inside, surprised when they went downstairs.

"Evidence is kept in the basement," Bella explained, her fingers whispering along the metal railing. "I wanted to check here first, since my desk is on the fifth floor."

Lunah's nails clicked on the cement stairs. Something banged and echoed in the dimness below. Markus frowned. "People work down here, in the dark?"

"Yes, there are several offices. File storage and supply are located on this level. If you need anything, pens, paper, a new chair, you go to the supply clerk." They reached the bottom and she pointed down a long corridor to the right. "It's down that way. File storage is also that direction and make a right. Evidence is this way to the left."

Smells funny down here, smells funny, Lunah complained.

Markus wrinkled his nose in agreement. Through their bond, the strong scent of mold, layers of dust, and the sharp odor of sewage assaulted his senses. He wondered if a pipe had sprung a leak no one knew about and hoped they were walking away from and not closer to the offending smell. Their footfalls echoed. Above their heads, thick pipes ran the length of the corridor. Every few feet a closed door broke up the unpainted block walls. Black stenciled numbers were on each door. He almost asked if they were holding cells of some kind. Lunah sniffed at the bottom of each door, sneezing when she inhaled dust.

What do you scent? he asked.

Old, everything is old. People, papers, fear, she answered.

Interrogation rooms then, perhaps. Bella disappeared into a wide opening before he could inquire. A small waiting space complete with chairs was divided from a chain link fenced off area that went so far back it disappeared into darkness. Rows upon rows of boxes and stacked files lined the expansive room. Hunched over a tall desk, a dark-haired young man flipped a page in a book. Long-burning lanterns hung from thick hooks on the posts for the chain link, casting enough light to see in the area, but nothing lit the deeper depths of the room.

The young man looked up when Bella approached his cage. He blinked behind glasses, his blue eyes huge. A grin split his face, revealing straight white teeth. A small patch of hair covered his chin. Markus ran his hand down his own long beard, the result of not shaving all winter. After learning he'd be arriving in Sziveria, he hadn't bothered. He was little more than a barbarian to these people, so he figured playing the part wouldn't hurt. The nation hadn't disappointed.

"Bella! What brings you down to my cave?" he asked. His deep voice still held the faint hint of youth.

Bella opened her bag and pulled out the file.

She set it on the long counter. "Hey, C.G., I need to see if you have the interviews for a case down here. I wanted to check with you first before I go searching through my files."

"How old is the case? They might be in long storage by now."

"I considered that. Could you tell me if they were?"

C.G. pressed his thumb to the hair on his chin and rubbed. "Maybe. My filing system isn't as detailed as long storage, but I can tell you if I had them to start with at least."

"Great." She flipped through her files and removed several sheets. She passed them under the small opening in the fence. "It's for these cases."

The clerk's mouth moved from side to side as he flipped through the top right corner of each sheet. "Okay, let me check. I'll—"

His voice died when he looked up and finally noticed Markus. He blinked again, his attention shifting to Lunah. A visible swallow bobbed the prominent Adam's apple jutting from his narrow throat. "Who ah, who's with you?" C.G. asked around another swallow.

Bella glanced over her shoulder and frowned. "Do you have to look so menacing?" she asked quietly.

Markus raised a brow. "I'm just standing here."

She sighed. "This is Markus Ralston and his

wolf Lunah, from Ruthenia. They're assisting in the investigation concerning Mina Endler."

"Ruthenian?" C.G. squeaked out.

Markus crossed his arms over his chest, and Lunah sat in front of him and licked her muzzle. "Don't worry," he said, making his accent thick, "Lunah has already eaten."

Bella touched the chain link dividing her from the clerk. "Ignore him. Please check on the cases."

C.G. took one more alarmed look at Markus before sliding off his stool. Taking down a lantern, he disappeared into the endless rows of evidence, a faint bobbing glow marking his progress. Bella sighed and turned, leaning up against the counter and crossing her arms. The action framed her breasts, showing him, *finally* the beautiful outline of her female curves. Small, less than a handful for him, but definitely the mouthful he'd wondered at earlier. He figured they'd be firm, and soft. Perfect. He licked his lips and dragged his gaze back to her face. She glared at him.

"Why did you scare him?" she asked.

The golden light of the lamps cast her rich hued skin in a bronze glow. Markus wanted to touch her. Wanted to pick her up and set her on the counter and settle between her legs and see how far she'd let a kiss take them. Lunah turned her head and snapped at the air, forcing his wayward, lust-filled thoughts back to the present.

"He expects a savage," Markus answered.

"So you give him one?" Disbelief rounded her eyes and filled her voice.

Markus shrugged. "Why not?"

"You want people to see you as uncivilized? Why not be the difference that creates a new opinion?" she asked, waving her hand up and down.

He narrowed his gaze and leaned forward. "Says the woman who hides behind a desk."

She leaned back. "I don't hide." When all he did was raise a brow, she scoffed and looked away. "I don't."

"I'm a beast master," Markus said, touching between Lunah's ears. "I'm not always civilized."

"You've been nothing but respectful to me. I don't see why you can't show that same person to everyone else," she said, shifting her weight, as though to admit his good-manners somehow revealed more than she wanted.

Markus took a step closer. "Maybe I want only you to see my *softer* side."

4

———————

Bella couldn't imagine anything *soft* about Markus, regardless of his confession. She almost laughed. Almost. But the challenging glow in his golden eyes made her swallow any words that might have formed. *Softer side*, yeah, right. In the fur-lined coat, with his long braid resting over his shoulder, and the beard, he certainly looked the part of a wild man. The only thing missing was a hatchet strapped around his waist and a sword at his back. Or maybe a bow. She squinted and tried to imagine which would suit him better. Either one would only enhance what he already had in an overabundance. Raw masculine appeal.

Lunah made an odd curious whining sound and tilted her head. Markus mirrored the motion. "What are you thinking?" he asked.

Heat blossomed across Bella's cheeks and she looked away. "N-nothing."

A very arrogant, satisfied male expression

crossed his face. Reyes had given her the same look when he'd caught her admiring him a time or two. Thoughts of her boss pulled her back into the present. She sighed and turned to see if C.G. had made any progress in his search. The faint arc of light on the ceiling far into the room let her know he'd at least made it to where the evidence might be located.

"Find anything?" she called, her voice reverberating off the cement walls.

A muffled, indiscernible answer sounded. Bella blew out a long breath and tapped her fingers on the wood counter. The glow of the lantern moved, flickering closer to the front. Bella straightened, nerves dancing in her stomach. C.G. appeared down a narrow row, papers in hand, and she had to stop herself from jumping with glee. He'd found something.

He set the pages down next to a clipboard, made some notes and then slid the board through the opening, tapping where she needed to sign. "You know the rules, returned—"

"Returned in a week, no alterations, no copies in place of originals," she recited, along with other redundant rules for evidence.

C.G. accepted the returned clipboard, placed all the evidence into a new envelope and handed it across to her. "It was all I could find. Hope it helps."

Bella looked at the envelope, excitement bubbling in her chest. "Thank you so much."

"Good luck."

Clutching the envelope in both hands, she turned and faced Markus, a grin spreading across her face. "Should we take this back to my house or to the arch guardians?"

"I did promise your mother I'd return for dinner."

Yes, he had. Because her mother had taken the time, and spent the raimarks, to put extra protein in their meal for him. Bella still didn't know quite how to feel about his kindness. He could have easily said he'd be unable to after their visit to the SNID building. Instead, he'd agreed to return, and eat whatever Madeleine prepared.

Behind her C.G. made a strangled sound. She glanced over her shoulder and found him staring, his glasses making his already wide-eyes look huge. "What?" she asked, unable to stop the defensiveness from entering her voice.

He held up both hands. "N-nothing. I just figured, you know, you were really selective about who you take to your mother. I mean, I've only asked you for the last three years to go out to a meal with me, or let me cook for you, or—"

Lunah growled. A deep, low, hair-raising rumble that had Bella pressing into the counter and which cut off C.G.'s words. Markus brushed his fingers between Lunah's ears, but never took his gaze from Bella.

Bella swallowed and took a slow breath. "Is she okay?"

"She's fine," he said, but offered no further explanation.

Bella glanced at Lunah and found the wolf staring at her, golden eyes intense. Licking her lips in nervousness, Bella turned her back to the pair and focused on C.G. "I've turned you down because you only see relationships for their short-term benefit, versus the long-term union I'm more interested in."

He propped an elbow on the counter and dropped his chin onto his palm. "Now see, why do you have to go and say things like that? You make me sound like I'm a man-whore."

"Because you are?"

C.G. grinned. "Maybe. But at least I'm a responsible one. Only contracts for me."

"And only for a year," she quipped.

"My second rule, after the first, which is you must be my wife to get you some of this." He waved a hand down his scrawny frame.

Bella shook her head. "And that's why I always say no."

"Well, you'll see when it's time to enter into one. Even a year commitment can be scary." A glimmer sparked in his big eyes and he smoothed hair from his brow. "Speaking of commitments, I'm meeting my next future contract in about an hour."

Bella's face twisted in disbelief. "What? When did your last contact end?"

"A week ago."

Rolling her eyes on a scoff, she turned and

waved in annoyance. "See you. Thanks again for the evidence."

"What? No good luck for me?" he called in disbelief as she walked out the doorway.

"You don't need luck, you need love," she cast over shoulder.

C.G. clutched his chest. "Don't curse me like that!"

Bella laughed, but didn't bother to reply. Lunah's nails clicked on the cement floor, adding to the whisper of Markus's booted steps. Bella wondered how such a large man could move so quietly. When they reached the lobby, Markus touched her elbow.

"We have one more stop to make," he said.

She raised her brows. "We do?"

"Yes. Do you know where your shield guardian... it is a shield guardian who is over this division, correct?"

"No, we have a master guardian. His name is Sullivan Oberon, and the ranked position he filled is of Master Guardian Perrella," Bella answered.

"I never understood why your guardianship ranking's carry a name not associated with the serving guardian," he said, moving out of the traffic path.

"It's to preserve our history. The first guardian to serve in the role Sullivan Oberon is currently in held the last name Perrella, and was assigned into a master guardian seat for voting rights in our Court of Laws."

"That is a nice way to remember heritage," he said. "I need to see him."

A niggle of unease flipped in her belly. "Why?"

"Do you know where his office is located in the building?"

Even if she didn't, the information would be easy to find. A directory at the front desk listed every guardian, ranked or unranked, that served within the building. Appointments were necessary, but requests for a meeting could be made. As a clerk, Bella knew the rules, and an unspoken one was a lowly worker such as herself did *not* show up in the office of the master guardian over the Haven City branch of the Sziverian National Investigative Division.

"Top floor."

"The greenhouse?"

"Well, sort of. He's located through the greenhouse. The greenhouse is open to every employee, but his office is inside."

Markus frowned. "Must be nice."

"I suppose. I don't think I'd want his job even with a greenhouse and city view."

Markus motioned for her to lead the way. "Something needs to make all that responsibility more appealing?"

"I'm sure for some the power of the position would be enough."

"But not for you?"

Bella shook her head. "No, not for me."

She opened the heavy door to the side stairs

not used often since they were fire stairs. The main steps were wide and could comfortably accommodate seven or eight people walking together. The fire stairs were lit only by windows at each switchback, which also contained a means of escape to the outside of the building if absolutely necessary. Bella preferred them to the crowded main passage, however. Less chaos.

Somewhere around the second floor, Lunah slipped by and took up the front leader position. The graceful wolf bounded up the stairs with ease, her tongue flopping from the corner of her mouth. Bella would show her one of the fountains when they reached the greenhouse, figuring that tongue would be rather dry by the time they arrived at the top level.

"Have you ever been in a marriage contract before?" Markus asked, his deep voice rumbling in the air around her.

Bella's grip tightened on the rail and she glanced over her shoulder at him. Curiosity lifted his brows and shone from his eyes. She returned her focus to the steps so she didn't trip and embarrass herself. "No. You?"

"No, not yet."

"Are your marriage contracts like ours?"

"Mostly. The end date can be left open and entered whenever the couple chooses, though it's rare for one to be filed."

"Why?"

"Most Ruthenians bond with their mate. It's a lifetime connection."

Bella bit her bottom lip. "Bond? Don't most spouses bond, though? I mean falling in love is a deep connection to another person."

"It's more than love."

What could be more than love? Bella frowned. "And this connection only happens between other Ruthenians?"

"Yes, it's unique to our genetics."

An unusual pain tightened in her chest. Nothing could happen between her and Markus. Not really. He'd be missing out on a key component to his marriage. And why the knowledge bothered her, she didn't understand. She'd known the man for hours, not days, or weeks. Not long enough for anything about his culture or relationship status to be of significance. And yet in that negligible amount of time, he'd treated her like no one else ever had. Like she mattered. His support in her talent, in her as a person, must be going to her head if she fancied notions of a future with him.

They reached the door to the greenhouse. The faint scent of earth and moisture seeped onto the small landing. Glass walls tinged green along the edges from algae growth showed the small oasis of nature. Markus's arm shot out and held the door closed before she could enter. Gasping in shock, she turned in confusion.

"What?" she breathed out.

He was so close his forest aroma mingled with the boxed earth fragrance of the conservatory. She wanted to lean closer, be surrounded by his heat and pure scent. Wanted to learn if he'd have any softness under all those layers or if he was all hard muscle and solid man. Bella pressed herself into the door. She'd *never* had such an insane desire before. No one had ever tempted her body or teased her mind with the possibility of what could be between a man and woman.

"You didn't want some meaningless one-year contract with a lover," he said as statement of fact, not a question.

Bella's gaze flickered to his mouth and back to his intent gaze. She shook her head, her voice stuck in her throat.

"Why?" He touched a loose curl near her temple, his knuckle brushing down her cheek to her jaw.

She swallowed against the dryness in her throat and took a moment to find her sanity. "My parents showed me how a relationship should be. The choice of love every day. Devotion even when things aren't... easy. Or even happy. A partnership, not something meaning nothing more than physical companionship."

His finger trailed along her jaw, sending odd butterflies into flight deep in her belly. "Some would argue that's the best part of a union."

"And they'd be denying themselves so much if that's all they cared about."

"Like C.G. has chosen to?"

Bella nodded. "Yes. I want more than C.G. could ever hope to offer me."

"Many would call you naïve for such a view."

She lifted her chin and squared her shoulders, despite her cowardly position braced against the door. "I don't care."

"And how do you plan to protect yourself from the wrong man if you're going to enter into a long-term contract?"

My mother. She bit her tongue to keep the knowledge to herself. Madeleine's genetic gift had already ensured her other children had married well in terms of how their prospective spouses matched them on an emotional level. Her mother wouldn't allow her to enter into a dangerous, potentially disastrous relationship. Sadly, Bella had learned the hard way if she told a man about Madeleine's gift, he'd try to learn if he had her mother's approval to be husband material. For some reason they believed her mother's positive insight meant an automatic permission to have her. After the third time, Bella had made her mother promise not to speak about her *feelings* about any man who walked through their door. Not that Bella brought any men home. She hadn't. Not for over a year. None of them had made her wonder at a future. Had made the risk of possible disappointment and heartache worth the effort.

Until now.

The sudden thought that maybe Markus Ralston would be different terrified her. She shoved it deep down inside. "Why do you care if I contract with the wrong man in my future?"

THE URGE TO KISS HER ALMOST OVERWHELMED Markus. Mere inches separated them. Leaning forward would close the distance. Would press his body to hers and he'd find out how soft all those hidden curves truly were. He'd learn if her lips tasted as sweet as she smelled. Instead, he took a careful step away. Despite the unique attraction he seemed to have toward her, Markus knew better than to think anything between them could go beyond a kiss. And since he feared he wouldn't be able to stop there, best to leave any intimate touching alone.

"I shouldn't care," he answered softly. "I have no right to concern myself with your future spouse."

She opened her mouth and then snapped it closed on a nod. Something close to confusion, or maybe disappointment, tightened her lips and flickered in her gaze. She turned before he could ask if his answer bothered her and snatched the door open with enough force to make the hinges squeal in protest. Holding the door for Lunah, he tried to convince himself letting the conversation drop was for the best.

A burst of humidity punched him. Damp and earthy, thick with the scent of mulch, composting dirt, and old water, the air barely moved under the glass panels rising two stories into the sky. Miniature trees brushed against the top panes, filtering the waning light of afternoon. Water bubbled and gurgled from fountains scattered around, bordered by benches. A pea gravel, brick framed trail separated and joined at various intervals. Bella led them to a low fountain and dipped her fingers in, looking at Lunah.

For me, is she doing that for me? Lunah asked, sitting and looking between the water and Markus.

Yes, I think she believes you're thirsty. Are you?

I am, yes, I am.

Then drink, he said, punctuating the words with a sweeping motion toward the fountain.

Lunah rose and sniffed at the water and then took a lapping taste. The water must not have been too terrible, for she began drinking in earnest.

"Will she be okay in here on her own?" Bella asked, wiping her hand on her pants.

Markus glanced around. A few birds twittered high in the trees, but otherwise the greenhouse seemed empty. "As long as it won't bother anyone to encounter her, she'll be fine."

"Okay, good, then she can wander while I take you to the master guardian."

Don't scare anyone, Markus ordered as he followed behind Bella.

Lunah yipped, but didn't dignify his request with an actual mental response. Markus shook his head. Stubborn wolf. Rocks crunched and rolled under his boots. In front of him, Bella fisted and opened her hands with each step, wiggling her fingers before repeating the process. Muttered words not directed at him floated on the air. The urge to soothe her nerves had him fisting his own hands. She wouldn't believe anything he had to say, he'd already tried to reassure her.

Master Guardian Perrella's office was a spacious glass room with only a single solid wall. Pulldown shades on the exterior walls made of glass could block out glaring light if necessary. Piles of folders littered the room. Loose papers were set on any available space. Frames peeked out from underneath tacked maps that were so marked over with various colored notes, Markus wondered how anyone knew what city, let alone country, they were seeing. Bella held the door open. Warm, dry air rushed past them, toying with the loose curls around her face and neck, and ruffled Markus's beard.

A man glanced up from behind a huge desk. Gold-framed spectacles perched on the end of his nose. He braced both forearms on the desk and looked at them over the top of his glasses. "Can I help you?"

Markus squeezed by Bella, unable to stop a shiver of awareness from sliding along his spine as his back brushed her front. How such an innocent motion could be enticing, he didn't know. Perhaps because he knew it was as close as he'd ever really be able to get to her. "Markus

Ralston, I'm the investigator sent by High Marshall Zan Veska to help with—"

"The Mina Endler case," the master guardian filled in. "I understand she was the daughter of a Provincial Marshall."

"That's correct."

The glass lenses flashed as he pulled them off, folding the ear pieces and laying them carefully on the desk. "I'm Sullivan Oberon, Master Guardian Perrella. I apologize for not greeting you properly downstairs. I was supposed to be informed of your arrival."

Markus lifted a brow. "In my country, when dignitaries, or other foreigners of importance arrive, someone is waiting for them. Sziveria has strange customs to me, so perhaps being on my own isn't such an odd thing."

Silence met Markus's words, followed by a long, uncomfortable sigh from the master guardian. "Two guardians were supposed to—"

"I've already seen the two guardians who were assigned to handle the investigation. I was taken to them several hours ago." He motioned to Bella. "Miss Fenwick has been helping me learn about the situation. Your guardians were not willing to do the same."

Sullivan's dark gaze flickered to Bella. "Is that so?"

"I'm not here to cause trouble. I wanted to personally request that she be assigned to work with me for the duration of my stay," Markus said. "She's not nervous around my wolf and as a clerk, her knowledge of the murders and evidence is beneficial."

"A clerk?" Sullivan asked in disbelief. "You'd rather work with a clerk than a guardian of our realm? An actual investigator?"

"I don't need an investigator," Markus stated. "I need someone competent. That is all. My high marshal wants answers and I plan to give them to him." *With or without your assistance.* The words weren't spoken, but their implication was clear and by the setting of Sullivan's jaw, he understood. "Since no one in any official authority has bothered to help, I'd rather continue on my own."

Sullivan leaned back in his seat and pinched the bridge of his nose. Gray hair shimmered in the darker brown of his short hair. "That's not quite how we do things here in Sziveria."

"So far, I have not been impressed with how you *do things*," Markus stated, anger making his words more of a snarl. "One of ours was murdered in your country. After seeing what your *guardians* consider evidence, I'd rather learn of the crime on my own. Be able to tell my high marshal without a doubt that the correct killer will be brought to justice who murdered the girl he considered to be a niece."

Bella's sharp intake of air hissed behind him. Sullivan's gaze shifted to her as he drummed his fingers on the papers.

"Are you okay working with this man?" Sullivan asked.

"Yes, of course, master guardian," she answered, no hesitation, chin held high.

Markus wanted to beam. Careful and guarded, he kept his expression neutral. For all the man in charge knew, he and Bella had only known each other for all of a few moments, not the hours they'd spent alone together. Stolen time.

Sullivan drummed his fingers again, looking between them. Clearing his throat, he stood and held out his hand to Markus. "Very well. Consider it done, Mr. Ralston. I'll expect to be kept apprised of any of your findings. I'd appreciate if you have anything of value to add that you also work with the assigned guardian team."

"Sure," Markus said easily, though he had no intention of doing any such thing. He planned to have the murder solved before they even figured out their plan to pin the murder on the wrong man had been discovered.

Sullivan squeezed Markus's hand enough to make sure he wasn't perceived as weak before releasing his hold. "Great. Was there anything else?"

Markus looked to Bella. She flushed and shook her head. Markus said, "No, I think that's all, for now."

Bella moved from the doorway and into the greenhouse. She clutched the strap of her bag in both hands, eyes wide. When the door swished closed behind Markus, she looked up at him. "I can't believe that just happened."

"Why?" He took her elbow and urged her to walk. "I didn't give him much of a choice."

"Still, you *should* be working with a guardian team."

"You heard what I told him. I meant it, Bella. *We* are the team. You, me and Lunah." The warmth of her seeped through the fabric of her sweater, tempting him to slide his hand to her fingers. He wanted the sensation of her bare skin. He snatched his hand free and let himself fall slightly behind. Enough to ensure he didn't acquiesce. "You are an acceptable loss, both to me and to him in means of losing personnel for however long I'm here."

She frowned at him over her shoulder. "Wow, thanks."

He growled. "You know I don't mean to undermine your worth. Rather, if I fail, I have no one to blame but myself, and he can say as much. I requested a clerk. Anything that happens from here on out reflects only on me, not on you or this division. Really, I just absolved the master guardian of any responsibility of finding Mina's killer. He's probably toasting himself right now."

Bella stopped and turned to face him. "Was she really your high marshal's niece?"

"Zan is very close to Mina's father. The loss was felt by many. The providence her father oversees was anguished when the announcement of her death was made public. There was a lot of outcry. I convinced the High Marshal to send only me when he requested my help, and if I felt more was necessary, I'd let them know."

She swallowed, her grip tightening on the strap until her knuckles turned white. "And do you?"

"Not yet."

She stared at him, her eyes moving over his face, as though she tried to divine the truth of his statement by what she saw. Markus wanted to ask if she trusted him. He met her gaze, looked deep into her ocean green eyes, daring her to question him, to voice her concerns. Her fears. Give him another reason to tell her she was important. Valued. She dropped her eyes and turned on her heel. Gravel scattered under her feet as walked away.

Markus swallowed a huff of frustration. *Lunah, we are ready to leave. Meet us at the exit.*

He caught up to Bella. "We have to use the door we arrived at, that is where Lunah will find us."

"Okay. I need to take another look at my files before we leave. I want to make sure I have everything pertaining to the cases."

"What about the evidence your guardian has?"

"Most of it concerned the wrong case. If we need anything else..." She lifted her arm and dropped it back to her side. "I guess you'll have to request it. I'm not sure what the protocol is for a situation like this one."

"We'll deal with that problem if we need to."

Lunah was sniffing at bushes near the door, half her body enveloped by waxy leaves. Chunks of bark flew out from under her belly. Markus frowned. "Lunah, *Zars'tka.*"

The wolf froze, paws braced, legs in a half crouch. Markus imagined her eyes looking away in guilt. Oh, yes, she knew better than to be digging. *You knew we were coming, you silly wolf,* Markus chastised through their bond.

She backed free. Leaves stuck to the fur on her back and a twig dangled from her ear.

"What did you say to her?" Bella asked.

"I told her to stop. A command. She must obey."

Bella opened the door. "Perhaps tonight you can explain more about how things work between you and your wolf."

Markus took the weight of the door from her, motioning for her to continue. Lunah did a full body shake, sending leaves, bark, and what suspiciously looked like cob webs flying. *What did you get into, Lunah?* he asked.

Her intelligent golden eyes twinkled up at him, while her pink tongue flopped from her mouth. Markus narrowed his gaze and frowned. Their mental link remained silent. Shaking his head, he motioned for her to precede him. She scuttled past, following Bella. They went down three floors, stopping on the landing with a big black painted 5 next to the door. Lunah sat and waited while Bella dug around in her bag. A silver key flashed moments before she slid it into the handle and the soft *snick* of a lock being released sounded in the silent alcove.

"You didn't have to unlock the greenhouse," Markus noted.

"The greenhouse is public. None of the other floors in the building are," she said, using her hip to push open the heavy door.

Lunah waited for Markus to take the door and Bella to walk by before entering. The door closed with a *thunk* against his back the moment he released his hold and followed Bella onto the fifth floor. Stenciled markers on the walls gave directions for what could be found ahead. The corridor from the staircase was empty, narrow and long, lit only by a window at his back and an occasional long-burning wall lamp.

Once again, Lunah took her place between them. Markus wondered if his wolf realized the significance of her actions. A smile quirked his lips. *Has the little Sziverian become important to you in such a short time?*

She is not among friends, she is not, Lunah answered, glancing over her shoulders at him. Her tail flicked and swished against his thighs.

I think you are right.

Her tail brushed his legs again. *You know I am, you know.*

Several turns and long corridors later, they arrived in the open space he'd been escorted to hours ago. Fewer people milled around. Most of the desks were empty.

"Where is everyone?" Markus asked.

"Day ends a half hour before sunset, to make sure everyone has time to get home before the ice arrives," she answered.

"Even in the warmer summer months?"

"No, in the summer work day ends at five. Even if we get late arctic winds, we won't freeze until after the sun completely sets in the summer, and even then, perhaps not. Is Ruthenia affected more by arctic winds?"

"Yes, we usually frost even in the middle of summer at night. But our plants have adapted. Our summer flowers still hold their blooms."

"I have seen paintings of your land. It's very beautiful. Rugged."

"Like the people. We are… untamed."

"But not savage."

"Mmm," he hummed, contemplating. "Perhaps some of our ways would be considered so."

Her forehead pinched in a frown. "For example?"

Markus shook his head. "No. Maybe when you know me better, I'll share some. Until then, I'm happy for you to believe I'm not barbaric."

5

———————

Steam rose from the bowl of bean and sausage stew Bella carefully set before Markus. Near the fireplace, Lunah ate without any grace or tact from a large pan of boiled meat and potatoes Madeleine had cooked of left-over bits purchased from the butcher. Sounds of snarfing and wet chomping filled the room.

Bella placed a bowl for her mother and herself and accepted a basket of torn bread passed across the short distance. All three bowls and the bread filled the table. Madeleine had grabbed a bedroom chair to make a third seat. Elbows bumped and apologies were issued all around as everyone adjusted in their seats.

Madeleine snickered, unfolding a napkin over her lap. "Well, aren't we all so polite?"

Bella stirred the floating herbs deeper into her soup. "I don't think you've ever entertained in this house, Mother."

Madeleine raised her arms and motioned

around the meager living space. "Entertain? Here? Most wouldn't even set foot onto this street, let alone be seen in this house."

And sadly enough, that included her siblings. In part because the pain of losing their family home, and the reminder of their father's bad decisions prior to his death, made entering The Rows difficult for Bella's older brother and sister. The other part was their inability to change the situation. They'd rather ignore the dire circumstance.

"There's nothing wrong with your home," Markus said between quick exhales across his spoon. "And this is delicious, thank you."

A faint flush blossomed across Madeleine's cheeks. "You're very welcome. Thank *you* for believing in my daughter. I will feed you every day for that alone."

Spoons clinking against bowls and faint slurping punctuated their small talk. Madeleine asked about the differences between Sziveria and Ruthenia. Bella remained silent, listening, sneaking glances to Lunah, who'd finished and licked at the pan. She wanted to pet the wolf again. To feel Lunah's soft fur under her fingers. To know the dangerous animal trusted her enough to allow contact. She didn't understand the odd urge, which was only a little less intense than the desire to touch the wolf's owner.

When she found herself almost giving in to the compulsion, she forced her hold to tighten on the spoon. A knowing smile tugged at her mother's lips, but much to Bella's relief, Madeleine stayed silent. The direction of her questions, however, took a different turn.

"Are you married, or promised to anyone, back home?" Madeleine inquired, unsubtle as only a mother could be and get away with it.

"No," Markus answered. "And I never have been. Finding a mate is a… process for my people."

"I have heard," Madeleine murmured, casting a sideways glance at Bella. "But you've made attempts?"

Bella pushed away from the table, picking up her half-eaten bowl. She didn't think — no she knew — she couldn't sit around and listen to Markus discuss finding a mate that could never be her. "I'm going to go water the greenhouse."

She poured out her leftovers in the compost bin and then set her bowl in the sink already full of soapy water. Pushing on the door to the greenhouse, the hinges creaked open. Warm, damp air stirred her curls and fluttered the edges of her shirt. A faint nudge on the back of her thigh made her look over her shoulder. Lunah stared up with hopeful eyes, licking her nose. Bella didn't have the heart to turn her away. She held the door open and the wolf walked past, into the small greenhouse large enough for two to work back-to-back among the shelved plants. Lunah sniffed at all the plants within her reach while Bella filled a row of large watering cans from a small spigot in the wall.

Above them, through the glass ceiling, a half moon and glittering stars filled the sky.

Starting with the highest level, Bella hefted the water can, allowing the water to rain down on the plants below. Soon water puddled and ran along the old mossy bricks beneath her feet. Lunah licked at the wet bricks. Bella searched around and found a terracotta catch pan. She filled and set it before the thirsty animal. Not caring about the damp ground, she crossed her legs and sat in front of Lunah. Licking the water remnants from her mouth, Lunah turned and met Bella's gaze. Slow, as if not to alarm Bella, the wolf lay on the ground and dropped her head onto Bella's lap.

Bella hesitated for a moment, then eased her fingers between Lunah's ears. The wolf's eyes closed and a sweet rumble rose between them. Cold water soaked into her pants. Bella ignored the discomfort, focusing instead on the warm fur beneath her fingers. Lunah's rough tongue rasped along her wrist. A tickle traveled up her arm and down her spine, making her shiver.

"Why do I want to pet you?" Bella asked, her voice a whisper in the quiet. "And why do I have this insane attraction to your master when I've only known him a single day?"

Lunah rolled onto her back. Her lips flopped open, revealing sharp, white teeth in an eerie grin, her head still cradled in Bella's lap. The wolf whined and wiggled, her front paws curling into her chest, her tail swishing. Water beaded along the short, pale silver fur covering her belly. Her ribs rose in sharp contrast. Bella chuckled and rubbed her fingers along Lunah's side. The sheer size of the beast once again astounded her. Stretched out as she was, Lunah took up the entire floor of the greenhouse. Bella imagined if she lay down beside her, they'd be near the same size, muzzle to tail.

"You are a big girl," Bella cooed, scratching harder when Lunah twisted and made happy sounds.

Golden light spilled into the small conservatory. Bella shied from the sudden brightness, squinting as a large frame filled the doorway. Markus stood unmoving, lost in shadows. He eased around his wolf, the door falling closed behind him. In the silvery darkness, Bella couldn't make out anything other than his massive presence. He sat across from her, hefting Lunah's back end into his lap and scratched at her haunches.

"Your *makyshka* said I can't stay much longer," he said, his voice hushed.

"Probably a good idea," Bella agreed, rubbing her fingers under Lunah's jaw.

"Lunah has never..." He ran his hand over the top of his head, and she had the impression that, if his hair had been unbound, he'd have buried his fingers instead. Her own fingers twitched at the thought of the feel of his long hair heavy in her hands. "She's not a social creature outside of our bond."

"You've mentioned this bond before. It's different from a dog and his owner?" she asked, hating the sensation her unfamiliarity with his gift caused. Markus was a mystery she wanted to solve.

"Much different." His head tilted back, revealing the masculine lines of his throat. "It's too late for this conversation, though. You'll have too many questions."

Bella gave Lunah one more chest scratch before tapping her breastbone. Lunah took the cue and rolled onto her belly. Bits of debris stuck to Bella's damp pants and she brushed them clean. Markus remained seated, Lunah's fluffy tail flicking free from his hand, only for him to grasp it again and let the length flow through his fingers.

"Are you allowed to discuss your talent?" she asked, unable to ignore his apparent unease with her curiosity.

"It's not a secret."

"But..."

He sighed and rose in a motion of fluid grace at odds with his huge frame. "But it's personal. Perhaps more than *you're* ready for."

Bella opened her mouth to argue, only to realize he might be correct. Personal meant sharing a sort of intimacy and if she were honest, no matter how much she might wish to know this man on a deeper level, only heartache would follow. She couldn't afford to be intrigued by him much more and think she'd survive without wanting the impossible. She nodded and took a step back until she brushed shelves, giving them room to move in the tight space.

"Will you meet me at the arch guardian's house in the morning?" he asked, gripping the handle of the door to return inside. "I'm going to review all the files you have and will want to go over what I find with you."

The thought of entering the Arch District was daunting and she had to take a moment to find her voice. "Arch Guardian Wolvenguard will be okay with that?"

"Yes. Why wouldn't he be?"

Bella blinked. "I'm—"

He cut her off with a hiss through his teeth. "If you say you're a nobody again I will kiss you to shut you up."

Lunah yipped. Bella had the oddest sense the wolf was agreeing with her master. The threat, or promise, had a curious sensation welling up deep in her stomach. Yes, she'd been kissed in her twenty-three years of life, but somehow she *knew*, Markus's embrace would be different. Dangerous. Bella clenched her jaw, thankful for the lack of light. "Fine. I'll see you in the morning."

"I'm not joking," he whispered. "If you put yourself down again, I'll take it as an invitation that you *want* me to kiss you. And I will."

Bella's heart pounded. Hard. Trying to burst right through her chest. She couldn't stop from pressing a hand to her collarbone in an attempt to ease the discomfort. Markus stood motionless, staring at her. Even in the dark, his gaze was hot, waiting for her to acknowledge his statement.

"O-okay," she managed to squeak.

The door opened and in a rush of fur and cloth, they were gone. Bella sagged against the sturdy plant shelves. Clay pots clattered and shook. She braced her hands on the cool, damp wood and took a long breath. What did Markus's warning mean? Did he want to kiss her and needed a reason? Or did he know she'd avoid such a scenario and therefore would bite her tongue when the urge arose to remind him of her position in society? She knew if she asked, he'd tell her, but she was too much of a coward, because what if he said yes. Yes, he wanted to kiss her. Yes, give him the reason.

That was how her mother found her, still cowering in the greenhouse, unable to face the brighter inside, where Madeleine might see more than Bella was ready for. Shadowed by the doorway, Madeleine braced a hip against the frame, arms crossed.

"I'm heading to bed. I have an early appointment. You might wish to come in as well, I doubt the flowers can handle much more watering," Madeleine said. "Markus said you're meeting him in the morning?"

"Yes."

Madeleine straightened. "Wolvenguard isn't

like the other arch guardians. His position isn't like the others, based on a rise to power. It's based solely on his ability to be a beast master and his agreeing to lead any other beast masters who come to work for Sziveria, which aren't many."

"But enough to warrant a role in our leadership."

"Yes, enough for that," Madeleine agreed. "But you don't have to feel like you're on a visit with the king elect, Bella. He's no different than Markus."

"Who knows his high marshal," Bella said, a lump rising in her throat. "I have a feeling he's an important man in Ruthenia, Momma."

"So?"

Bella shook her head. Her mother would lecture her more than Markus if she stated, again, how unsuited she was to be helping on the investigation. "Never mind."

"Mmmhmm," her mother hummed in that motherly way that said she knew her daughter had been on the verge of saying something asinine. She looped her arm around Bella's shoulders and guided her to the door. "You are important, too. Some day, child, you'll see that."

"I DID A TIMELINE LAST NIGHT AND DISCOVERED something interesting," Markus said the second Bella was shown inside. No preamble, no chance to look around the behemoth of a residence. To take in the gleaming dark marble, a staircase bigger than her house leading to the second and third floors, or to catch a glimpse of what the rooms off the cavernous foyer held.

Markus came rushing at her, papers fluttering, hair damp and unbound, shirt untucked, feet bare, looking far too good so early in the morning. The dark length of his hair fell in a long, glossy sheet down his back and over his shoulders with no hint of curl. His maroon shirt was unbuttoned to the center of his chest, revealing a dusting of dark hair and masculine lines.

Bella managed to tear her gaze from his relaxed appearance. Tried not to imagine how much more disheveled he'd look after rolling out of bed, or how much less he'd be wearing. "Was there not a timeline already in the file?"

"No, there wasn't. Perhaps your boss... what's his name again?"

"Guardian Reyes Avner," Bella answered.

"Perhaps Avner has one in his office, but there wasn't one within the cases." He didn't slow down as he led her toward the back of the house. His legs were longer, eating up more space than she could manage without running to keep up. "Since we added cases that weren't originally part of the investigation, I would have had to do one anyway, though."

"True," she conceded.

"The timeline I discovered makes your theory even more sound. They all fit."

"All the murders?"

"Yes." He stopped at a set of double doors in a huge, nearly empty room. Only a few pieces of thick rope, fitness equipment, and a narrow stone wall in the center of the room with objects jutting from it at various intervals took up any space. The east and north walls were glass. One looked out over the property, the other into the greenhouse. He opened one of the doors into the conservatory, ruffling his hair and shirt.

Bella followed him out, to a graveled area with a large low patio table surrounded by padded furniture. A neat breakfast was arranged on a platter, untouched. The rest of the table was covered in papers, a notepad, and colored pencils. Sunlight spilled in through the high vaulted glass ceiling. Birds twittered and called. Bugs sang. The foliage was so thick and untended, Bella couldn't see more than a few feet into the expansive glasshouse.

"Wow, why is it so wild?"

"It's not used for food or florals, but for training. Both wolves and the teams that will work with them," Markus answered, sitting and spreading the papers he'd been carrying in front of him. "Here, look at this."

Bella tore her attention from the dense indoor forest. Her curiosity would have to wait. She perched on the short couch across from him and waited for him to explain his findings. The buttery scent of pastry and sweet cut fruit had her swallowing back hunger. Markus pushed the tray across to her without a word. Bella glanced up at him, but he wasn't paying her any attention. How had he known? She pulled the tray closer and tore off a chunk of flaky bread.

"Thank you," she said, popping the savory pastry into her mouth.

"You're welcome. I had it brought out for you, I already ate." He looked up, a smile toying at his lips. "You struck me as the type to sleep until you're forced to run out the door."

She laughed. "How could you possibly have figured that out about me?"

"Your mother let it slip to be kind to you in the morning. You'd either be still waking up, or grumpy, maybe even both." The smile curved up one side of his face, making his dimple appear. "I figured that meant you usually skipped breakfast, which might account for any grumpiness."

Bella had forgotten Markus and her mother had been left unattended, and Madeleine liked the beast master. Any inquiries made by him would have been answered if they weren't too personal. He turned a paper around with columns of dates, names and how the flower had been found on the victim. She touched that column and glanced up at him in question.

"Since you'd decided the way the victims were displayed and the flower were a common factor, I thought I'd include it in my list," he explained.

"Ah," she said and continued reviewing.

Something about the dates teased her mind. "Nothing in the summer months."

"I noticed that as well. Also, the dates of the first and last murders within each year feel significant."

Bella chewed on the inside of her bottom lip. "We should go to the archives and look at seasonal information, see if anything fits. Maybe it's the day the leaves changed or something."

"That's a great idea." His attention shifted to the forest for a moment before returning to the documents in front of him. He gathered together the timeline, some notes, and a handful of colored pencils, and held them out to her. "Would you mind?"

She took everything from him and deposited it in her messenger bag. "What about Lunah?"

"She's going to remain here, in the greenhouse. I don't know how the archives would react to her presence."

Bella stood and adjusted her bag. "I think since she's *your* wolf, they'd not say much at all."

"Perhaps, but why risk it? She's happy running around. Nick is here, with his wolf. She enjoys playing with other wolves when she gets the chance."

"She plays well with others?" Bella asked, surprised.

"Yes, though she's very alpha and I have to watch her when she meets someone new, that she doesn't fight for dominance."

Bella imagined Lunah in a fight, all bared teeth, aggressive growls, and bunched muscle. A shudder raced up her spine. "I suppose that would be bad."

He shrugged. "I don't allow it to ever reach a point where it could be."

She followed behind him through the dim interior. "Hired carriages don't come to the Arch District. We'll have to walk a bit to find one."

"I discovered that yesterday, after I arrived. They won't even wait at the entrance." He pulled boots on, and then held the front door open. "Nick would let us use his driver, but his need to leave the residence can be sudden, so I declined."

"I wouldn't have agreed to it anyways," she said before she could stop herself.

He raised a brow. "Why not?"

Bella stared at him. When he still looked at her in confusion she gestured to the massive residence. "Arch guardian."

Markus squinted, craning his neck as he glanced up at the house. "Yes?"

"His carriage would be clearly marked as such, I can't be seen getting out of it. Things would be... said." She shook her head and jammed her hands into her coat pockets. "No thank you."

He continued to frown, falling in step beside her. "Things?"

"I'm considered gen-common, Markus. The

reasons for me to be in his residence, let alone getting out of his carriage, would be limited."

"But you'd be with me, and I'm here for a specific purpose, and no one even knows who I am."

"Still, it's not worth the questions or speculation."

A heavy sigh left him. "You worry too much."

Bella figured she worried just enough. "My job—"

"Is important to you, I know."

They walked the rest of the long street in silence, the brisk wind a constant companion. Sparse traffic flowed at the main road leading deeper into the city. Markus signaled for a carriage, surprising her when one actually stopped. Bella gave the address to the archives and climbed in while Markus held the door. The cab rocked heavily as he climbed in and settled his frame into the small space across from her. Their knees almost touched. The crisp rain and forest scent of him made the cramped space seem even smaller. No matter what she did, she couldn't escape his presence.

He sat forward and reached around his back to gather his hair together. Bella clasped her hands, wanting with an uncomfortable desperation to touch the length. Would the strands be coarse, or soft? His elbows bumped into the sides and top each time he tried to weave a braid. Frustration pinched his face and rumbled in his chest.

"Do you need help?" she asked.

"I should have done this before we left, but I was too distracted about learning more information."

"You could leave it down," she suggested, appreciating how unguarded he looked.

He shook his head, giving no further explanation.

"All right," she ventured, "then let me help before you hurt yourself or have a lopsided braid."

Using his fingers as a comb, he undid the plaits he'd managed. He unwound a leather tie from his wrist and held it out to her before giving her his back, kneeling on the floor at her feet. Air caught in Bella's throat. Her hands trembled as she gathered the strands together, starting at his forehead and combing her fingers through. Thick, heavy, and soft enough to make her want to play with his hair for hours, the faint sun glinting through the windows caught on the rich wine-red shade with each twist she made. The finished braid fell halfway down his back, and she wound the tie around the end several times before knotting it off.

"Finished," she whispered, forcing herself to let the braid fall between his shoulder blades and not to touch him anywhere else. Resisted sliding her hands over his broad shoulders, to the heat of his bare skin underneath his shirt.

Kept herself from pulling him back, where it'd take little effort to move forward and lean enough discover how he tasted. His skin. His mouth. She kept very still, her palms pressed to her thighs.

He rose and returned to his seat, pulling the braid over his right shoulder. "Thank you."

She cleared her throat and drew a line on her chest. "You might want to…"

Blinking, he glanced down at his partially unbuttoned shirt and laughed. "Ah, yes, thank you."

The carriage slowed to a stop in front of the archive building. Thin cement supports framed glass walls two stories high and almost a block deep. Only open during daytime hours to eliminate the need for flame powered light, the almost entirely glass building glimmered in the morning light. Inside, a row of guides waited to help patrons. Bella told them the information they needed and followed when an elderly woman rose and led them deep into the first floor, among rows and rows of files, ledgers, and bound tomes. She explained the file system and then left them to their research.

Hours later, surrounded by weather patterns, seasonal progression charts, and catalogued sunrise/sunset times, Bella found herself overwhelmed. "You do this for every case? All this research?"

"If necessary," he said, scribbling yet another mundane fact on a notepad he'd smiled to procure from one of the sweet old ladies up front. Smiled. Not growled or menaced. Bella had wished she'd had a notepad to part with, too, just to see it again. His smile did funny things to her inside. "Solving crimes isn't all action and chasing villains through the streets."

"I know that." After all, she was the one who filed all the information away for later use, if necessary.

He shook his head with a small smile. "And yet you seem surprised by our research."

Bella looked over the stacks of data and sighed. "I guess I don't understand it's purpose, now that I'm here. What can we possibly learn?"

Markus stood, pad in hand, and came around to sit beside her. The feet of his chair screeched on the floor as he scooted close enough for their shoulders to touch. He flipped his braid to his other shoulder and angled his frame to face her. His elbow braced on the table, pencil touching the paper at the top line of the table he'd created.

"See this?" he asked. "These are the temperatures, highs and lows, for each murder. What do you notice?"

"Moderate day, freezing at night."

"Correct. He's only murdered when Sziveria experienced more than a frost. It had to be *frozen* outside. That really narrows down when he decides to make his kills."

Bella looked over the facts. "He's accelerated."

"Yes. One murder his first, second and third year, two his fourth, three his fifth, and now in his sixth year, he's already murdered three times at the start of spring. If his trend continues, he'll murder at least one more time in the fall, before winter fully sets in."

Bella frowned. "But doubtless more."

"Yes, if what I've recorded is correct, more is probable."

She drummed her fingers on the pad. "Do you think he's hunting now? Finding who will be his first victim once the temperature falls?"

"I don't know what these girls had in common. I don't know what motivates him to choose them to answer that." He gathered all his notes together.

"Or the significance of the below freezing temperatures."

"Right. We know it's not for preservation, he's making sure they're found before a full day passes."

Bella organized the table. The ladies had made it clear they were not, under any circumstances, to return the items themselves, but she felt guilty leaving a disorganized mess.

"Mina was murdered two weeks ago," Markus said, "is her apartment still a crime scene?"

"I don't know. The address is in the file, we can go look."

"Will we need a key?"

"I have credentials. We can ask the manager to let us in."

He raised a brow. "Go to a lot of crime scenes?"

"No. I need identification to get to my desk, especially if someone new is working the front counter. Everyone who works in the building has some sort of identification showing we belong and aren't a random visitor trying to sneak around."

"Ah, of course."

She shouldered her bag. "Ruthenia doesn't have official credentials?"

"I'm sure we do, I however, have never needed any, so it's not something I think about."

Bella contemplated his statement. "Everyone knows who you are on sight?"

"No," he said carefully. "Everyone knows a beast master on sight. Show up at a location with a wolf and everyone assumes you've been asked to be there."

"Hmm," she hummed. "If only things would be that easy here."

6

———————

MARKUS STOOD IN THE CENTER OF MINA ENDLER'S living room, hands on his hips, sorting through all the various little things he remembered from her file. Where she'd been found lying. Where her possessions, which were now safe on a ship bound for Ruthenia, had been located. The tiny apartment was empty, for the most part. A table with two chairs was in the kitchen. In front of a window overlooking the street three stories below sat a rocking chair coated in a fine layer of dust. A bare mattress on a frame took up most of the space in the bedroom to his left.

The landlord admitted it would be months before he could rent the small apartment. Mina's death was too new. No one wanted to live where a young woman had been murdered. As a result, little — except for her belongings being removed — had been touched since her death. Bella hovered in the entryway. Her toes scuffed at the brightly colored woven run under her feet.

"What are you looking for?" she asked.

He did another turn, taking everything in, his fingers drumming on his hips. "I'm not sure. Something."

"Do you think the killer's scent is still here?"

"After all the people who have been in and out of here, Lunah would never be able to separate the scent without knowing it first."

Bella moved around the kitchenette, nothing more than a single counter, a woodstove and a small sink with some shelves above. "Why was Miss Endler in Sziveria?"

"She was studying at the Haven City Academia for Art." He wandered to the set of windows. "She admired one of the artists who taught and convinced her father to allow her to attend."

Markus leaned against the wall between windows, crossing his arms over his chest and looked out over the steady flow of traffic. "Sziveria isn't exactly a high crime destination. Not like Perazil or Mark Inland."

Bella joined him at the window. "We have enough crime to warrant three prisons and three correctional facilities."

"I happen to know those three prisons in the Northern Boundary house more than just your criminals. Most of Sziveria's law breakers end up in the much nicer correctional facilities, while the violent criminals of the inhabited world make their way to the brutal and freezing cliffside prisons up north."

"Yes, that's true," she conceded, leaning her shoulder on the wall and letting her head drop to rest on the window frame. "She should have been safe here."

"Being targeted by a serial killer is something no one could have anticipated, and is no fault of the country. Her father will understand that in time. But he needs answers."

Bella nodded. "I hope we can get them."

A flutter of movement caught his attention. Straightening, he touched the bottom of the window. "Does this open?"

Bella touched the edges, slid her fingers into strange indents along the frame and with a grunt, began pushing the glass panel up. Markus helped. Cold air rushed inside.

"What is it?" she asked.

"I'm not sure," he muttered, leaning his head outside. His shoulders bumped the small frame. He angled to be able to reach outside. A small flower box, filled with dirt and decaying leaves, was bolted to the brick exterior just below the edge. Brisk wind swirled around him, disturbing dead flowers in a small glass vase. Mindful of the three-story drop, Markus eased the bouquet inside.

Bella hummed at the discovery. She reached, but stopped short of touching the withered petals. "How odd that they were sitting out there."

"How long do you think they've been dead?"

Bella shrugged. "I'm not sure. We can find a Gen-Heir botanist, they might be able to tell us."

"It might be helpful. If they fall into Mina's timeline, this could be important."

"Especially with the dead flower being left on the victim. We should find out what kind of flowers these are and see if the one left behind matches any in the bouquet."

"The botanist can tell us that, too."

"This is a good find," she said, smiling.

"It'd be an even better find if something similar were found at other crime scenes."

Her face scrunched in contemplation. "I don't recall anything being said, but then again, I don't know if anyone checked anything outside."

Markus resisted the urge to growl. "A crime scene is more than just where the victim is found."

"I know, but I doubt anyone thought to look outside the window like you just did. In fact, you weren't looking for anything when you found the flowers."

"True, but I'm not the lead investigator. If I had been, I'd have checked the windows, the hall, the alley, and the greenhouse…"

Bella glanced around the vacant apartment. "Perhaps you can teach them something, then. Anything else?"

"Yeah, I want to look in the other rooms."

He handed the vase off to her and then searched the bedroom, small closet and bathroom, which reminded him of a compact train bathroom, complete with the shower housing the sink and toilet. Nothing else caught his attention. Bella waited for him next to the front door, the decaying flowers clutched in both hands as though afraid she'd drop the evidence.

For a moment he was struck by her beauty, like a lightning bolt straight to his gut. Never before had a woman caused such a strong reaction in him. Sure, he found all females to be beautiful. The opposite, softer, but not always sweeter, half of man. Something about Bella was *different*. He wished he could figure out what exactly. Except what would he do then? Already he denied their genuine attraction, did everything possible to prevent acting on any desires. If he learned why she drew him like a magnet, he doubted he'd do much different. He *wanted* her. In a way that terrified him because the truth was too hard to ignore.

Bella could be his possible mate.

A Sziverian. The thought was too absurd. Yet, there she stood, an undeniable temptation to his inner beast to lay a claim. To make *his*. Markus drew in a ragged breath and tore his gaze from her.

"Did you find anything else?" she asked, oblivious to his self-contained distress.

He shook his head, not trusting his voice. If she were Ruthenian and they were mates, she'd sense his stress, she'd know deep within he was upset. Even if he somehow managed to convince her to give their relationship a try in the future, could he forego the closeness he'd obtain from one of his own kind? No answer came forth. Not that it mattered. Now wasn't the time, and for sure not the place, to be worrying about something unlikely to happen.

"Do you know a botanist?" he asked, shoving his anxiety aside.

"I don't, but my mother will."

Markus raised a brow and she laughed.

"She knows everyone," Bella explained, holding the flowers out to him. "A lot of people have trusted her with their relationships over the years."

"That could be very useful." He accepted the vase. "Does Avner know of Madeleine's connections?"

"No, why would he? I'm his file clerk. We don't discuss much outside of work."

Markus stared at her. Avner was a bigger idiot than he suspected. "How do crimes get solved in this country at all?"

Laughing, she opened the door into the narrow indoor corridor outside the apartment. "Guardian Avner treating me as any other employee doesn't keep crimes from being solved."

"He has an untapped resource in you and he doesn't even know it because he doesn't talk to you."

Discomfort pinched the corners of her mouth and reflected in her eyes. "I'm okay with him keeping a professional barrier between us. I've seen what happens to careers and reputations when that line is breached."

Markus wanted to argue that there was more to Avner's lack of attention. She was stunning, and intelligent, and to the guardian who likely aspired to achieve a ranked guardianship at some point in his career, she was a peon. A nobody. To him, she offered nothing useful except to make sure his cases were filed in a correct manner. What a waste. Markus would not be making the same mistake.

"Is your mother home?"

"I have no idea of her schedule today." A faint flush darkened her cheeks. "She was already gone when I woke up."

He smiled at her admission. She waited while he made sure the door locked behind them. "We'll return to Wolvenguard's then and see if the type of flowers left behind have been mentioned in any of the notes, and to get Lunah before going to your place."

Curiosity shone in her eyes as she held the door open for the stairs. "You think the bouquet really matters."

"I do. If the killer has left any behind at the other scenes and someone noticed, he might have already been caught."

"If they're from the murderer," she pointed out, sighing.

"We'll find out soon."

· · ·

HAYDEN JOSSERN FLITTED AROUND THE HUGE greenhouse like a butterfly seeking the perfect flower. Employed by a wealthy merchant, the Gen-Heir botanist oversaw the elegant work of a talented indoor landscape architect. Bricked paths, stone benches framed by lamps, fire pits, and fountains created a living sanctuary envied by anyone who had permission to step inside. Prized Wintervail orchids were located in their own special section, complete with a sign and directions on how to find them. Come Wintervail, a huge party would be thrown to share their blooms, welcoming in the bleak, cold season ahead with a celebration of gifts and color. Bella had never seen the flower in person, out of season or in bloom, and her curiosity was making her antsy.

Each plant the botanist walked by, he touched and then made notes on a clipboard he carried. In fascination, Bella observed leaves stretching for Hayden's touch, curling around his fingers when he finally brushed by them. Markus followed a step behind, his patience waning if the tense frown on his handsome face was any indication. Lunah pressed her nose to the back of Hayden's thigh, causing the short, thin man to jump.

"Oh, oops, hello again. Sorry. I get lost in my plants and forget people are around me, too," he rushed out, hugging the clipboard to his chest. Dirt caked under his fingernails and darkened the lines of his skin. He gestured to the thousands of plants surrounding them. "They're all seeking my attention. My work is never done."

"We won't keep you for long," Markus's deep voice assured. He held out the vase of dead flowers. "I just need to know what you can tell me about these."

Hayden glanced at the flowers and then at Markus. "They're dead."

"I know that. Can you tell me how long and what kind?"

Hayden searched around and then took a few steps and set his clipboard on a cart with seedlings. "Of course." He motioned for Markus to set the flowers down. One by one, he eased the stiff stems from the tangle, laying them out in a neat row. "They withered like normal, but have been frozen. You have daisies, carnations, amaryllis, which is interesting since they're out of season at the moment, so very expensive, marigold, and poppy. A simple arrangement that would have had lots of color."

"How long ago did they die?" Markus asked while taking notes.

"I can't tell you that so much, but I can tell you they were cut around three weeks ago. They began dying at that point." Hayden brushed a finger along the edge of several petals. "You can see some crystallization here on the larger flowers, an indication of having been frozen. Since we're still getting frosts, likely multiple times if they were outside."

"Thank you." Markus went to reach for the bunch and Hayden held up a hand.

"Do you want me to get some paper to wrap them in? Trying to stuff them back into the vase will lead to breakage."

Markus looked at Bella, his brows raised in question. Bella's mind blanked. No one ever asked her opinion, or felt she had one of value. While this wasn't the first time he'd looked to her for input, an actual decision involving the case was far above her role. Sweat broke out across her palms and she rubbed them on her thighs.

"You can submit them for evidence in any state," she said.

Not a true reply, but information. He could make his own choice for how much he wanted to preserve them. Markus narrowed his gaze. Yes, she knew cowardice rang in her non-answer, but she'd not be responsible for something so important.

"Wrap them," he said, still looking at her. "Please."

Hayden found a gardener and sent her to retrieve a sheet of brown paper to wrap the dead bouquet. Bella turned away, taking in the lush conservatory. Unlike many others that had tall trees, the owner had decided instead to have hanging vines and ferns draping from suspended planters, giving the space a fantasyland feel. Exotic birds flitted around in bursts of vibrant color, kept safe and warm inside. Bella wished she had time to sit and watch them. To take in the lush greenery. Allow the serene beauty to calm and renew her.

Lunah watched a gathering of birds at a shallow bath. The predator lurked in her eyes. Every muscle in her frame went still. Not even her ears moved. Bella sighed and touched the wolf's nose with a light tap.

"They are not snacks, and we're guests," she chastised.

Lunah stretched out her front paws and yawned, showcasing her thick canines. She sat and turned away. A clear message that while she'd heard the order, she didn't have to like it. Bella chuckled and scratched between Lunah's ears.

"One more thing," Markus chimed in, holding up his pencil. "Do you know of any flower vendors that would sell the amaryllis?"

"Not specifically," Hayden answered, carefully wrapping the evidence. "But you'll likely find one at Extilis Square, where the money of the city shops."

"I can take you," Bella told Markus when he looked her way. "The largest book store in the country is located there, I go as often as I can."

Markus thanked Hayden and then used a hand motion to catch Lunah's attention. Together, they walked from the greenhouse. Bella kept her disappointment internal at the missed opportunity to see the Wintervail orchids. She tried to crane her neck to catch a glimpse, but only foliage and decorations were visible. The greenhouse extended far beyond her view. Huffing a quiet sigh, she accepted the weight of the thick glass door from Markus, making sure Lunah's tail was clear before allowing the door to close.

Gloom filled the mansion attached to the greenhouse. Bella imagined a tomb felt about the same. None of the extravagant life from the conservatory graced the interior. Empty glass vases sat on pedestals below massive paintings of bleak landscapes. Bella shivered and wrapped her arms around her waist. A footman in grays and blacks opened the front door for them without a word.

Bright sun and the rumble of traffic made Bella blink in shock as she stepped outside. Markus had already hailed them a carriage by the time she could see well enough to navigate the wide stone steps down to the sidewalk.

"Mr. Harold's Book Emporium," she told the driver as she accepted Markus's help into the carriage. The thrill of his fingers along hers made her want to hold tight. She released him the moment she stepped foot inside.

Lunah bounded in after her, settling on the threadbare carpeted floor. Markus closed them in and squished himself into the seat across from her, setting the package next to him on the seat. Bella shifted to the right to make room for his knees. The carriage rocked into motion and she looked out the window, the huge homes of the rich easing past.

"What are you hoping to find at the flower vendor?" she asked.

"That they keep detailed records of their clients," he replied, the pages of his note book rustling as he flipped through. "If they don't, someone remembering something would be helpful. Have you ever been along for an investigation?"

"No, why would I?"

He shrugged. "If you allow yourself the freedom, you have great insight. I'm happy you're along."

A flush heated Bella's cheeks. She squirmed. How was she going to return to a desk job and be satisfied after he left? The thought of him leaving darkened a different part of her heart. She didn't want to think about the day when he'd step aboard a ship and sail back to Ruthenia. "Well… thank you."

Lunah licked at her paws, catching Bella's shoes with each swipe of her raspy tongue. The ride to the square didn't take long, the wealth of the area having spawned the prestigious shopping destination decades ago. The driver stopped at a line of carriages taking on and letting passengers out in front of the three-story building an entire block in size. The sidewalk in front of Mr. Harold's bustled with activity. People walked by carrying brown paper wrapped packages or colorful crocheted tote bags heavy with purchases.

Bella took the package from Markus and waited for Lunah to hop down before following. Markus paid the driver and then they wandered the bustling sidewalks in their search for the flower vendor. Bella spotted the quant storefront between a dressmaker and a cigarette shop. A wooden sign on a hanger swung in a lazy arc. The painted bright yellow flowers and golden letters for Flowers of Haven City flashed in the sun.

A little bell tinkled when Bella pushed open the door. Draped in colorful fabric, from strands braided into her hair, wrapped around her shoulders and waist, falling in elegant folds to her ankles, a woman with darker caramel skin than Bella's greeted them with a warm smile.

"Afternoon, welcome to Flowers of Haven City. What blooms can I find for you today?" Her accent was unique, one Bella hadn't encountered before, lilting with emphasis on the vowels.

"Afternoon," Bella began, "I'm Bella Fenwick, and this is Markus Ralston. We're here on behalf of the SNID for an investigation."

"Oh, my." The woman touched a hand to her full chest. "I'm Marlise, one of the owners. How can I help you?"

Bella held out the paper wrapped bouquet. "We're hoping you can tell us about these flowers. A botanist said you might sell amaryllis out of season?"

Curiosity shone in Marlise's eyes as she accepted the flowers. "We do, yes, along with a dozen other rare blooms for this time of year. Very popular among our patrons."

Markus joined Bella at the counter, his notebook opened to a clean page. "This bouquet would have been ordered around three weeks ago. Do you keep records of your purchases?"

"We do," the florist said, unwrapping the paper. "Some of our customers are very picky about their arrangements always being the same, if possible."

"You'll be able to tell us about this arrangement, if you made it, then?" he asked.

"Oh, yes, I made this. See this one?" She held up a stem of small dried gray flowers. "It used to be very bright blue, very bright. I've bred them special in my greenhouse, and you can only buy them from here." She motioned for them to wait and disappeared into the back through a swinging wooden door. Moments later she returned carrying a handful of brilliant blue sprigs. "See? When paired with pinks and yellows, the blue is the star, even so small."

"Beautiful," Bella agreed.

"This bouquet had white amaryllis with the softest of pink lines and tips. The blue was a good choice. If I remember correct…" Marlise shook her index finger in thought and looked around under the counter. "Ah here we are, yes.

If I remember correct, this customer always designs his own arrangements."

"He's been a patron here a long time?" Markus asked.

Marlise laid a thick bound book on the counter and flipped halfway through. Her long fingers skimmed the pages. "For years now, yes."

A bubble of excitement formed in Bella's chest. "Anything you can tell us would be helpful."

"If you give me a moment, I can show you the history of his orders."

"Do you know his name?" Bella inquired.

"Yes, though I don't think we have a complete card on him, just his name and where in the order book we can find his past arrangements. Do you have time?"

Markus smiled. "We have time."

An attendant lowered lamps hanging above the table in the greenhouse, pulling Bella from her deep focus on the case files spread out before her. When had the sun began to set? She glanced around, shocked at the darkening depths of the indoor forest behind her.

"Oh, no, I didn't send my mother a message," she said, unable to keep the worry from her voice.

"I did, don't worry," Markus said. "What have you found?"

She blinked and stared at him. When he didn't look up, she took a calming breath and reached for her notes. "According to the botanist's reports on previous victims, the flower found on the victims were a daisy, carnation, orchid, daisy, orchid, rose — which is the only one that stayed as a form in the victim's mouth — primrose, primrose, orchid, daisy, and Mina was another carnation."

"And the rose is the only variant and it stayed intact, but he didn't use it again. How odd," Markus murmured, stroking his beard. "You're certain of the rose being our suspects crime?"

"You saw the drawing," she said holding her hands open.

"Yes, indeed." He flipped through his notes. "Okay, Flowers of Haven City only has nine documented orders from him, which means he had to use a different florist possibly two times."

"Maybe he wanted something different for those victims, something Flowers didn't offer, or maybe his budget didn't fit with them," she offered.

"The budget theory is good," Markus said, pointing his pen at her. "According to the dates for victims eight and nine, and the flowers that he purchased from the Extilis Square shop around the window for their murders, the bouquets were much smaller. Only around ten flowers total."

"So, he used someone cheaper for murders

six and seven, obviously wasn't happy, and returned to Flowers of Haven City, but spent less on the arrangements to stay within his budget."

"Yes, I like that." Markus scribbled notes. "Maybe he didn't want the flowers to stay intact. Maybe you have it wrong that he wanted it to, since the rose is the anomaly."

Bella considered that. "Why crumble them?"

"I don't know. They come from the bouquets though. We can confirm that based on the orders and the botanist's reports." On a sigh, Markus leaned back, taking the pen in both hands and pursing his lips. "Okay, here's what I have. He orders a specific arrangement, somehow gets his victim to accept the flowers, and kills her within a week of ordering them. The flowers we found were placed outside, and we have no reason to think he hasn't done this with the others."

"Where, since he only kills when we have below zero temperatures, he wanted them to freeze," she surmised.

Markus pointed his pen at her again. "Yes, excellent. And the dead flower in her hands and her mouth is significant, too, but I don't think we'll learn why until we find him."

"We have a name."

"Yes, now we need to look through witness testimony and see if someone interesting keeps showing up."

Bella narrowed her gaze. "Someone interesting? How do you mean?"

"Habits of the victim. Did they all visit the

same coffee shop? The same dressmaker? Did they all end up taking a ride from the same driver at some point? Did any of them receive any deliveries from a specific delivery agency? Go the theatre within a week of their death? Those types of things."

Bella thought back to all the reading she'd conducted on the case when she'd realized Guardian Avner's error in suspects. "Mina took regular walks in the park near her apartment complex the moment the snow melted enough. She went to the community theater every month."

"All local things, and none of the other victims overlap Mina's habits." He grasped the pen in both hands again and brought it to his chin. "Keep thinking."

She studied him. "You already know. You found it, didn't you?"

"You will, too."

Bella shook her head. "Nope. Tell me."

Groaning, he leaned forward and tossed his notebook at her. Bella caught the fluttering pages, careful to keep from ripping them. She flipped through his scratchy writing, skimming his thoughts, surprised at his organization. Her brows raised. "A delivery man?"

"Every witness claims to have seen the victim receive a delivery at least once. Sometimes twice, when the flowers arrived." Markus relaxed back in his seat again. "Mina received a small order of art supplies she'd purchased before the arctic winds set in that finally managed to arrive two weeks before she died. I'm going to visit the shop in the morning to find out what delivery service they used for her order."

Excitement warred with nerves. Bella eased the notebook onto the table. "Guardians Avner and Hinke are going to fight you on this."

"I know, but if I need anything, such as a letter of accusation to be able to search his home, I'll go to Master Guardian Perrella. I'll have enough evidence to ask for his support."

Bella stood. "I hope you get it."

"You'll be coming with me," he said, rising.

"Markus…"

He held up his hand. "You deserve to see this through to the end. Don't you want to?"

Bella tapped her fingers against her thigh and looked beyond the ring of light around them, her heart in her throat. Yes, she wanted to see Markus finish the case. To see the suspect capable of causing pain to so many families brought to justice. "I don't want to cause issues."

"How could you? Aren't you keeping me organized?" He waved his hand around. "Helping me keep from losing things?"

Laughter bubbled from her. "Is that how you're going to explain it?"

"Since you won't let them see you as anything more than a clerk, who am I to force you to ruin the illusion?"

Bella didn't know whether to be offended or grateful. "Thanks."

"Be ready in the morning. Lunah and I will pick you up at the corner of your row and Beekman Avenue at eight."

"Not in the arch guardian's carriage, I hope."

Markus smiled.

7

Haven City Delivers was a large enterprise, occupying the entire third floor of a five-story building, sharing the structure with lawyers, accountants, architects, and a host of other civilian services. In addition to the occupants who kept the delivery business busy, the surrounding businesses also used the active courier service. They employed over a hundred delivery personnel, a number that had impressed Bella. If she weren't mistaken, they were the largest courier service in the city, possibly the country. She hoped they kept good records of their jobs.

Markus spoke in hushed tones with the office manager, while Bella and Lunah lingered at the back of the managers office. She watched through the windows overlooking the busy floor. Boxes, envelopes, and paper wrapped bundles were handed off to shouting delivery staff vying for the next job. The manager had explained the employees were paid on a per delivery basis. The more they made in a day, the higher their wages. None were assigned, it was on a first to accept basis. By how swiftly orders were running out the door, there wasn't a shortage of objects needing to be distributed.

"Birk Volken is out on a delivery." The manager pulled a sheet of paper free from a pad. "This is where I've shown he should be."

"I'll need his delivery record for these dates," Markus said, handing a sheet of paper to the manager.

"We pride ourselves on being discreet," the manager said, frowning.

"I don't need the what, just the who. If I require more, I'll get an accusation letter requesting the information from the SNID."

The older man flushed at the mention of the Sziverian National Investigative Division. "Has he really done something so bad?"

"I'm not able to discuss anything," Markus said.

"Of course, how silly of me," the man rushed on. "We've never had any complaints against him, nor do I have notes that he's missed a delivery, or possibly stolen property to be delivered."

"All things I'll be sure to take note of myself," Markus promised.

Bella raised her brows. In effect he'd made the manager think Birk was being investigated for theft, not anything more serious, like murder. If they were lucky, the man would keep his mouth shut about their inquiry. If he didn't, Markus was going to have to move fast to make sure the suspect didn't disappear on them.

Close to an hour later, the manager handed Markus a stack of light blue slips. "These are all the jobs he took in the time frames you asked for."

"Thank you. Do you have an office we can use?" Markus asked while Bella accepted the papers.

The manager motioned for them to follow and led them to a small space with a desk and two chairs. "We're in between floor recorders. This would be their organizing space after a shift."

Markus thanked him again and closed the door. Bella set the papers down and moved to make room for Lunah along the side of the desk.

Markus split the paper stack in half. "You look for the names of the women in this pile, I'll look for them within these." He set the paper with the women's name between them.

Bella pulled a chair closer and sat. Lunah settled between them, her rear under Bella's feet, and her shoulders under Markus's. Halfway through, Bella's shoulders began to ache and her stomach growled. She cleared her throat to try to mask the sound.

Markus flipped a sheet onto his *read* pile and made a note. "I knew I should have fed you after we left the artists shop."

Perturbed, she twisted and stared at him. "I'm fine."

"I know you're fine. I know you aren't starving. I know you'll be okay until we leave. All the same, I also know you didn't eat before you met us at the street corner." He caught her gaze, brow lifted. "Right?"

Once again, she found herself unnerved by his easy knowledge of her. She looked away, focusing on the delivery slip in front of her. "I've found four of the victims so far. You?"

"Five." He sat back in the seat, dropping the pen on the desk. "It's enough to take to Master Guardian Perrella."

They'd confirmed ten of the eleven women had been delivered to by Birk Volken. The eleventh was likely among the receipts they still had to sift through.

"Do we need to try to find the last woman?" she asked.

"Yes. Every piece of evidence matters." He sighed and retrieved his pen. "I can't help wondering how many of the women we've set to the side might in fact be missing."

"Since he likes his victims found, perhaps we're lucky and none."

He made a noncommittal sound and kept flipping through pages, making notes. Bella watched him for a few seconds before shaking her head and returning to her dwindling stack. A deep whine left Lunah as she rolled onto her back, paws curled into her chest, head titled until she looked at Bella. Using the toe of her boot, Bella scratched Lunah's belly.

"She's ready to leave," Markus said and tapped his temple. "She is whining in multiple places."

Bella laughed. The sound died in her throat as she read the final name of the victim they'd been looking for. She held the slip toward him.

"Ah," he whispered. "There she is."

Bella clasped her hands between her knees. "What happens now?"

Markus organized all the receipts back into a single pile. "Now we see how serious your SNID is about catching this guy."

MARKUS LEANED AGAINST A METAL BEAM supporting the glass wall overlooking the greenhouse in the master guardian's office. The consistent rustle of papers being turned broke through the tense silence. Beside him, Bella stood hunched into herself, rubbing her thumb along her jaw. Her gaze hadn't left the guardian since he'd started searching through the evidence they'd amassed.

"I don't see Birk Volken on the suspect list," Perrella said.

"He wasn't," Markus replied. "All the evidence for how I came to the conclusion he's the killer is there."

"Yes, thank you. I'm surprised the assigned guardian team didn't find any of this. From the art delivery, to the flowers." Perrella sighed. "They missed too much."

"A delivery was noted in the file for the fifth victim. However, she wasn't associated with the original case," Markus pointed out.

"Noted and not followed up on." The master guardian shook his head. "Six cases since that could have been avoided if your research is correct and you find proof of guilt at his residence like you're hoping."

Markus straightened. A thrum of excitement coursed through his veins. "You're going to give us an accusation?"

"Yes, I'll get an accusation letter written for permission to search his residence. Use a corner radio if you find what you're looking for and need an immediate letter of custody. I want him at the nearest Haven City Enforcement Services building in custody if you do."

"What do we do until then? How do we keep him from running?" Bella asked. "If he knows we suspect him and we don't have the letter, how can we detain him?"

Master Guardian Perrella braced his forearms on the desk and clasped his hands. "As you know, in Sziveria, the evidence of guilt must be established and the burden of proof falls to us. He's considered dangerous, and therefore we can detain him once we have the proof required for custody, where he'll remain until his accusation hearing."

"I understand that," Bella said, patience tight

in her voice. "How do we keep him from running while we're finding the proof?"

"You will need to watch his residence and enter when he's not present and doesn't suspect anything. He should go about his life normally. If you find evidence, that's when things will change. If he arrives while you're still searching, you show him the letter giving you permission to be present and ask him to sit and wait until you're finished."

"And that works?" she asked, her face twisted with skepticism. "The guilty sit and… wait?"

Markus hid a snort with a cough. Not in his experience. The guilty always ran. Self-preservation. Fear. Fight or flight always emerging as flight.

What do they do without beast masters, what? Lunah asked.

It sounds like the guilty often run loose, or they get lucky a lot.

There will not be running, there will not.

No, Markus agreed, *there won't be.*

"We don't often run into problems when the guilty are approached. We are civilized, after all," Perrella answered Bella, steepling his fingers. "The few instances of aggression don't warrant changing our methods."

Bella blinked. "What kind of aggressive instances?"

The master guardian waved the words away with one hand while holding a paper out with the other. "Nothing to worry about. Go find your evidence."

Markus took the letter, giving it a cursory glance before handing it off to Bella. "Thank you."

"I will be the one thanking you if things go like you believe they will."

Finger gesturing their farewell, Markus held the door open for the ladies. Bella's attention was on the document. Markus grasped the back collar of her shirt, guiding her onto the path before she walked into a tree.

She stopped in the center of the trail. "What if we don't find anything? What if he's some creepy stalker, not a killer? Or what if it's a complete coincidence that he's delivered something to all these women?" She turned and grabbed the front of his jacket, the paper crinkling in her hand. "What if the killer is following *him* and our theories are wrong?"

Gently, he peeled her fingers from his clothing and squeezed her hands between his. "That's why we investigate. Why there is a process. We can only go where the evidence leads, and right now, it's leading us to Volken. If he turns out not to be who we're looking for, then we start again, find a new thread, and see where we go."

"You're very calm," she said, her pulse racing a visible thrum against her neck.

Markus narrowed his gaze. The usual rich caramel shade of her beautiful skin had become alarmingly pale. "And you are not. Come here."

He reached for her, tucking her into his side. The length of her frame settled against him. The urge to swing her around and see how she'd fit when held to his front forced his eyes closed. Desire didn't flee, instead he envisioned her wrapping her arms around his waist, her hips aligned with his, her breasts announcing their eagerness for his touch, her lips seeking his in delicious ways. Her faint tremble of anxiety over the case brought him back to the present, and why he'd touched her. He found a bench and took the few steps forward, depositing her on the seat.

"Lean forward, slow breaths in and out. Steady," he instructed, holding the back of her neck to make sure she obeyed.

"I'm sorry, I don't know what's wrong with me."

"Fear," he said, massaging along her neck. "You are afraid we will fail, and what that'll mean for you. Don't worry, I already told you I've taken complete responsibility for the case. If anything is wrong, you are of no fault."

Her fingers wound around his. "I want you to be right."

Markus dropped to his haunches in front of her and touched under her chin, his thumb tracing the curve of her bottom lip. Summer sun, but he wanted to taste her. He waited until her ocean green eyes met his stare. "All that matters is discovering the killer. We will achieve our goal, one way or another. Being right or wrong has no consequence until we find the next piece to the puzzle that is uncovering the murderer. Even being wrong will provide us with necessary answers. We will have eliminated a possibility and can search for the next one."

She swallowed and took a slow breath. "I think I prefer filing."

Laughing, Markus stood and helped her rise. "I enjoy the thrills of investigating. The solving of a tangled mystery."

She released his hand and tried to fix the crumpled letter. "I hope I didn't make this unofficial."

"Nope, it could be covered in mud and would still be legitimate," he said, taking the paper. "Let's go find the evidence we need."

Dust motes danced in the air, sparkling each time they encountered a thin shaft of light penetrating through the closed curtains. Stale breakfast scents lingered. Fried bacon. Burnt toast. The bitter hint of a peeled orange. Bella took in the small studio living space. The twin bed tucked into the wall, surrounded by shelves, with drawers under the mattress. A paper covered window and drawn curtain provided a dark cubby for the sleeper. A long line of counters took up the left wall. Worn and sagging, a single recliner with a tray for eating was the only furniture.

Uneasiness made her fidget at invading someone's personal space. Despite being a suspect for multiple murders, a person lived his day-to-day life in the room. Safe. She figured the victims found in their homes had felt much the same. That at no point would anyone violate the sanctity of their residence. Bella drew on that to force herself into a different mindset. They needed to catch this guy, and the only way was to find evidence he considered outside their authority, therefore hopefully in plain sight.

Lunah sniffed around the room. Markus opened a curtain along the back wall. White light flooded inside, illuminating the walls covered from the ceiling to within a few feet of the floor in floral artwork. Watercolors, oils, drawings in colored pencils, highly detailed charcoal sketches in various sizes canvased the place.

"I guess this is where his money is going," Markus said.

Bella started at the door and eased her way around the room, inspecting each piece of art. "Incredible." She pointed to a sixteen-by-twelve oil painting. "This is a Georgie Kraymer original."

Confusion twisted his face. "Who?"

"Only one of the most famous still life artists of this century. He was one of the first documented artists to have a genetically inherited talent for art in our country. The moment he picked up a brush at age three and looked at a daffodil popping up between bricks in his family greenhouse, he could paint it with precision required by years of training. He just…" She snapped her fingers. "Knew. The knowledge was there for him to draw upon. Turned out his great-grandfather was a Ruthenian, though no one could confirm the creative gene since anything to do with the man was still in Ruthenia."

Markus crossed his arms over his chest and regarded her. "Then how did he have a great-grandson in Sziveria?"

"Oh, you know, some sordid tale of seduction so popular among speculators. His family hasn't shared, but many others, including a small biography at the Sziverian Museum of Art, say he traveled here for inspiration, impregnated a Sziverian, returned home not knowing of his progeny, and the rest is history."

"This art of his, it's expensive?"

"Yes, and sought after." She shook her finger at the detailed painting showcasing a bouquet of bright pink blossoms in a crackled glass vase of colors fading from blue hues to green. "I bet this is why he couldn't afford the more expensive flowers for three of his victims."

Markus removed his notebook from his jacket pocket and made quick notes. "I should have asked for a scene artist to come with us."

"Georgie only uses one gallery to sell his work. Finding out when it was bought, and by who, should be very easy. All his other works are at museums around the world."

"Does he teach?"

"I'm not sure. I think it'd be hard for a Gen-Heir to teach, don't you? They already know what to do, how could they explain an inherited gift to those who don't have the same talent? You could inquire at the art school, though."

Markus shrugged. "It would have been another thread to follow to connect Volken to Mina if he's obsessed with this artist and Mina was in Kraymer's class."

Bella took in the rest of the art. "I don't think he's obsessed. I think perhaps an opportunity to purchase the painting arose and he took it. The rest of these are of great quality, but he doesn't have another Georgie Kraymer. After the cost of everything here, he could have afforded to buy one or perhaps even two more, but he didn't. He continued collecting other works."

Markus's pencil scratched on the paper. "You know a lot about art."

"The museum is free," she said, smiling.

"And with your talent, I suppose I shouldn't be surprised." He returned her smile, though the gentle edge startled her. "How many art pieces at the museum have you managed to sneak in a touch?"

She flushed. "A few."

He stepped close enough to trace a simple carved frame hanging near her. "Oceans and forests?"

"And the imaginings of buildings before the cataclysm," she admitted. "Huge glass structures that went so high into the sky you couldn't see the tops." Closing her eyes, she remembered being transported into the heart of an ancient city street, surrounded by monolithic columns of steel and glass. "We can only imagine how breathtaking such an experience was for those living among so much splendor. The steel necessary alone is astounding. To have such excess for transportation *and* building to inconceivable heights? Yes, I wanted to see."

"There are still some ruins on Miami Island," he said.

"I have heard, along with the shells of strange vehicles that could once fly. Fly!" She shook her head. "I don't think I could have climbed into a steel body and risen into the sky."

He laughed. "Yeah, I don't think I could have, either."

Bella glanced around the small room. They were on a time limit and her distraction of art was costing them precious minutes. "What do we look for?"

"Anything that connects him to the victims." He motioned with the pencil around the room. "This art is fantastic since we have the confirmed flowers, but it's not enough. We need something linking him without question."

The shelves flanking the sunken bed and the small shelves within the enclosed space caught her attention. Lunah followed her to the bed, sniffing the mattress and curtain. Bella's knee sank into the plush blankets.

"This is the only place he seems to have anything personal," she said.

"I'll check his bathroom."

Leather and paperbound tomes rested in haphazard stacks on each shelf. A small collection of pencils and pens had her leaning forward in interest. Did he draw? Being surrounded by so much art, she could see how Birk would be inspired to attempt to recreate the flowers he seemed to love so much. She grasped as many narrow books as she could hold and pulled them down in front of her. Sitting half on the mattress, she opened the top book and gasped. A journal. The dates were written neat and precise in the upper right corner of each page. Yesterday. He wrote daily.

Bella's hands trembled as she flipped through the pages looking for a specific date. Her breath caught when she found the entry. Explicit and charged with emotion, Birk detailed his feelings for Mina Endler. Starting from when he touched her at a delivery, to his obsession and eventual need to murder her.

"Markus!"

He poked his head from the bathroom, took her in, and rushed to her side. "What? What have you found?"

"Journals." She waved to the stacks taking up the narrow bed shelves. "Look, dozens of them. I bet there's more on the other shelves. He writes daily, and look." She held the diary open to him. Tears from excitement mixed with sorrow burned in her eyes. "Mina."

Lunah whined, sitting close enough to touch Markus while he turned pages with increasing speed. An anguished groan left him. "He killed her over dead flowers."

Bella swiped a tear away, opening other journals until she found the next date she needed. She shook her head in disgust. "He killed Janine Hennings for the same reason. I bet they're all here. Every murder."

The book snapped closed between his fingers. "We need nothing else. Find a bag to pack up all the journals and I'll go radio Master Guardian Perrella. He can send a SNID or HCES guardian to level the accusation and bring in Volken."

She jumped up, anxiety spiking hard through her chest. "You're leaving me here?"

"Lunah will be with you, and I'll be on the street corner." He paused at the door. "Don't miss even a single journal. Look through every book if you have to."

The door closed with enough force to shake the frames on the wall. Bella looked at Lunah, who titled her head to the side, whining. "Yeah, I feel that way, too."

"Okay," Bella breathed, rubbing her hands on her thighs. "I don't know the protocol here. Can I find a bag to use inside the apartment? Or do I need to go find someone and ask for one?"

Lunah didn't have an answer. The folded letter from Master Guardian Perrella crinkled in her pants pocket and she pulled it free. "What does this say?"

After reading the perimeters of what she could and couldn't do, Bella went in search of a bag. Anything she needed to obtain evidence in a legal manner was at her disposal. She needed a bag. Searching through drawers, she found a set of canvas sacks. She pulled out two and then went to work filling them with the diaries. Door hinges squeaked, the sudden noise taking her by surprise.

"I'm almost done. What did the master guardian say?" she asked, shaking the bag to see if she could fit another journal in along the side.

Lunah's soft growl sent goosebumps along Bella's skin. Alarm jolted through her and she slowly turned, a journal clutched in her hand. A short, pale man not much older than her, with medium brown hair, stared. His mouth was open, his grip tight on the doorknob.

The killer.

Out of instinct, Bella took a step back and connected with the mattress frame. She tumbled backward. The bagful of books toppled over and spilled onto the floor. Before she could scramble up, the heavy weight of the man landed on her torso, locking her hips to the mattress, and pressing into her shoulders. Bella shrieked and reared, kicking her legs and twisting her shoulders. His face turned red as he put more of his bulk onto her, his forearm pressing hard into her collarbone.

"You have no right to my journals!" he yelled, spittle flying onto her face. "Those are mine! Only for me!"

His arm slid to her throat, choking her. Bella clawed at his arms. Panic seared across her nerves and she tried harder to dislodge him. In the corner of her mind detached from the horror of being asphyxiated, Bella realized every woman he'd taken from the inhabited world must have gone through the same sense of dread. The knowledge of knowing he was stronger and determined to steal her life.

A high-pitched bark morphed into a deep throated growl. Bella stopped attempting to cause harm to Birk and instead reached for Lunah, her fingers grasping at air. How she wished she were capable of communicating with the wolf like Markus, to shout for help with nothing more than her mind.

Sharp claws dug into her thighs a split second before Birk let loose a shrill scream and toppled off her. A thump joined Lunah's harsh growls, echoing off the walls. Fabric tore. Birk begged bet ween screams, pathetic pleas for mercy. Bella touched her throat and tried to swallow, sucking in deep lungsful of air.

The door burst open. Wild-eyed, Markus took in the scene. In two bounding steps, he crossed the room and dragged her, still heaving for breath, into his arms. One hand clasped her head while the other wrapped around her waist and held her tight to his body. Bella accepted the need to be held and returned his hug. Under her cheek, his heart beat a rapid rhythm, matching her own racing pulse. His beard tickled her forehead.

On the floor, Lunah lay atop Birk, her tongue lolling and eyes bright. Birk raised his trembling hands, but made no other motions.

"An enforceman should be here soon," Markus said, rubbing gentle circles along her back.

She tried to move out of his arms, but he tightened his grip. "I have to finish packing up the journals."

"They can get them." He tucked his index finger under her chin and pushed her head back. His fingers brushed the tender column of her throat. "Are you okay?"

Bella grasped his hand, lacing their fingers together. "I'm fine. Really."

"Lunah, *dokhor vok*," Markus whispered.

The wolf yipped.

Bella laid her cheek on his chest, keeping a tight hold on his hand.

"What did you say to her?" she asked.

"That she's a good wolf." He rested his cheek on the top of Bella's head. "She told me when Birk arrived and what was happening. I ran back as fast as I could."

An exquisite sensation traveled through her. Safe, warm, surrounded by his scent of rain drenched forest, Bella figured she could remain in his embrace forever. "Your link travels that far?"

"Our link doesn't have a range, at least not that I've discovered."

Questions filled her mind, but Birk whimpered on the floor, reminding her that now wasn't the time to ask them. Bella pulled herself from Markus's hold. He let her go, his fingers slipping free of her hand. Irrational disappointment made her frown. The heavy pounding of boots in the corridor pulled her from her discontent. Bella edged around Lunah and Birk to the spilled journals.

A male and female enforceman entered the small apartment, followed by Guardian Reyes Avner. A journal fell with a heavy *thud* from Bella's hand. She snatched it up and shoved the thin book into the bag.

Hands in his pockets, the SNID guardian took in the scene. "So, you think this is the serial killer?"

"We don't think anything," Markus stated, crossing his arms over his chest, accenting his larger size. "The journals Bella found will give you all the information you need. I'll write a report tonight for your master guardian to sign and approve to take to my high marshal."

Avner held his hand out. "Thanks for your assistance."

Markus regarded Avner's hand for a second before accepting. Bella kept her sigh of relief internal. Rising, she clutched the bag of diaries to her chest. Lunah bared her teeth when Avner took a step closer. Avner froze.

"No moving," Markus instructed, his attention on Birk. "Or she sinks her teeth into you again, understand?"

Birk nodded, his head bumping the floor. Lunah rose and went to Markus's side. The two enforcemen worked in quick unison to secure the suspect. Bella eased closer to Markus as they pulled him into a standing position.

"Can we go?" she whispered, knowing her request painted her a coward and not able to care.

Avner stepped into their path. "I'll take the evidence."

Markus held his arm in front of Bella. "No, guardian, you won't. We will be taking this to the Investigative Division ourselves. I've already made arrangements with Master Guardian Perrella. You can use the corner radio to confirm if you need."

Avner's jaw clenched. He nodded and moved to the side. Markus urged Bella through first, Lunah trotting behind him.

"You know he'll take credit for the custody," Bella said the moment they were out of earshot.

"Yes, I know. I don't live here. My career is not in Sziveria, so I don't care if he claims credit." In a surprise gesture, he slung his arm around her shoulders and pulled her close. "We know the truth, and a killer is off your streets. This is all that matters."

Bella knew he was right, and still knowing only she and the master guardian would be aware of Markus's role in protecting their city chafed. Or perhaps her unhappiness came at knowing with the crime solved, he'd be re- turning home.

EPILOGUE

PORT SCARBROUGH
  Two days later

SEAGULLS DRIFTED IN THE SKIES ABOVE. EACH aerobatic dive they made was accompanied by a long croon. Markus shaded his eyes against the glare of the sun, watching the birds with trepidation. Nothing ruined a day like getting crapped on. Since sailing away from Bella already counted as a ruined day, he didn't need anything more added.

The ship destined to carry him away creaked and groaned a boarding plank away. Waves lapped at the hull and broke against the seawall and pillars. Lunah whined and lay on the stone walkway built from the barrier.

I don't want to go, I don't, she grumbled.

Did you not tell me we were here for one thing?

Well, we've solved that one thing and it's time to return home.

What if I want here to be home, what if?

Bella crouched and eased her fingers through the thick fur between Lunah's shoulders. "Don't like to sail, hmm? I don't know if I would either."

"You've never sailed?" Markus asked, shocked. Though, considering where she lived, he figured he shouldn't be.

She continued to pet Lunah. "No. I've been on the MagnaRail to go visit the beaches and cliffs in the south, which was amazing, but not a ship. Too many places in our nation my parents wanted to see when they had the time and funds to travel."

"I can understand that," Markus admitted, his attention on the bobbing ship. "There are places I've not seen in my country and I should."

Lunah whined again and rolled onto her back. *I don't want to go, I don't.*

Annoyance flared through Markus. He didn't want to leave either, and having her echo his displeasure made him want to lash out. But there was no fault in how either of them felt. An interesting challenge had arisen at his meeting Bella. He wasn't ready to admit fully how deep the dilemma ran, but the seed had been planted all the same. He had no doubt in the coming months, even separated from her, something beautiful would sprout.

Bella stood, her gaze on the ship. A gust of wind buffeted the wool of her jacket and whipped her dark hair around her face. She pulled strands from her mouth and stepped closer to him. "Will you write when you arrive in Ruthenia?"

"I said I would." He patted his front jacket pocket. "I have your address and the transmission code for the nearest public radio station to you."

She folded her arms, tucking them in tight to her chest. "Is it unprofessional of me to say I'll miss you?" She glanced down at Lunah. "Both of you."

"We are no longer bound by any professional standards, if we ever were. I do not work for your government," he said, moving closer and sliding her hair over her shoulder and behind her ear. Her tongue slid across her full bottom lip, leaving a glossy, far too tempting trail. Markus caressed down her arm to her waist and drew her into his body. "I really want to kiss you."

Her eyes widened and she pressed her mouth closed, nostrils flaring. She searched his gaze. The wild beat of his heart stuttered. He'd never been unsure of the welcome of a kiss, and while he couldn't claim to know her well, he knew her enough to know she'd accept a kiss on her terms alone.

"I really want to say yes," she whispered.

Markus brushed his knuckles under her jaw, tilting her head back. "But?"

"I'm scared. A kiss from you…" Her eyes fluttered closed. "Would be dangerous."

"For both of us," he agreed. "However, it's just a kiss."

She touched his beard, his chest, and down to his arm. "Is there really such a thing as *just a kiss*? In my limited knowledge, a lot rides on the experience, including expectation."

"I don't have any expectations."

An almost sad smile touched her lips and glimmered in her eyes. "Maybe I do."

Before she could object, he brushed his lips to hers. A fleeting, all too quick stolen kiss. He grasped her chin and met her shocked stare. "When I return, and I'm going to Bella Fenwick, you will let me kiss you exactly how I want to."

THANK YOU SO MUCH FOR READING! CONTINUE ON for a sneak peak at the next installment for Bella and her beast master – *Perfect Melody Silenced*.

PERFECT MELODY SILENCED

Sneak Peak

Releasing February 7th, 2023

Port Scarbrough, Sziveria
September, 801P.C.E (Post-Cataclysmic Event)

Among the faces in the crowd awaiting the ship docking from Ruthenia, one was missing. Markus Ralston frowned, disappointment a sharp jab in his chest. Beside him, his Ruthenarc wolf Lunah jumped up and down, trying to see over the half wall.

Where is she, where? Lunah asked through their bond.

I don't know, Markus answered, leaning forward and resting his arms on the rail.

She knew we were arriving today, she knew?

Yes, she knew.

He'd sent Bella Fenwick a letter, and a radio message, letting her know a Sziverian family had contacted him to investigate the death of their daughter. Markus's assistance in April finding, and apprehending, a serial killer had led the desperate couple to seek him out and offer a reward for any information he could obtain concerning their daughter. Without a second thought, he jumped at having a legitimate excuse to return to the country.

To return to Bella.

The ship eased into position at the dock. Workers jumped into action attaching the plank for disembarking. A small group cheered on the wharf. They waved a pink banner and shouted. Seagulls dove and caught currents on their search for anything edible dropped by the people waiting. Their cries mingled with the ocean waves breaking on the wharf.

Markus and Lunah waited until the bulk of the passengers had gone ashore before venturing down the plank. The crowd had thinned to a few stranglers watching the ship for the passengers they awaited. Enough people had left to confirm Bella was indeed not present. Bag slung over his shoulder, Markus considered his next move. Ignore her lack of appearance and go meet the family hiring him, or seek her out.

On the way to the train station to go from the port to Haven City, his imagination went wild. Perhaps the scrawny *boy* behind the fence in evidence had finally managed to convince her to give him a yearlong marriage contract. Or the man she worked for, Guardian Reyes Avner, had wizened to what he'd had in front of him. Letters and radio messages couldn't compete with flesh and blood. By the time he hopped into the railcar, he'd managed to convince himself she had a line of a marriage contracts waiting.

She is ours, she is, Lunah stated, her words calm and certain.

We've been gone months. A lot can happen in that time.

No. She punctuated the single word with a loud bark.

Markus sighed and scratched the top of her head. "We shall see."

No one sat beside him, not with Lunah at his feet, large and imposing. His silver and slate gray wolf stared anyone down who slowed, her golden eyes alert. As a Beast Master, he was awarded privileges where his animal was concerned. Their bond connected them on a physical level. When he concentrated hard enough, he could smell, hear and if she were far enough way, see all she did.

The train jerked into motion. Iron and steel squealed and grumbled. The release of brakes hissed. Markus swung his bag into the empty seat next to him and focused on the Sziverian land sliding past his window. Untamed forest broken by rocky fields, with the occasional small city. Subtle reminders of humanity's endurance nearly a millennia after an event history still hadn't uncovered almost managed to extinguish their race. Harsh arctic winters, and the arrival of a deadly sexually transmitted virus known as human rabies syndrome, served as continual reminders of life's fragile condition. Of the importance of living the gift given to each generation born in a world offered a second chance.

Markus didn't plan on squandering the potential future he'd found in Bella. Not that Lunah would allow him to. Despite all they both had to lose in a union outside of their own heritage. Over the long summer months separated from her, Markus had come to the conclusion only an outright rejection would stop him from pursuing the remarkable Sziverian. Even then, he'd figure a way to convince her to give them at least a year. The country had a funny way of doing relationships, but he'd take her any way he could get her.

Nature gave way to warehouses for the products being brought in from the ports to eventually be distributed through the city and country. Warehouses transitioned into homes and businesses, coming closer and closer together until Haven City, the largest city in the country, formed. The train slowed at the station, bustling with people. A sprawling glass canopy rose over the station, keeping rain or snow off the patrons, but not warmth inside. Enclosed vendor booths provided an escape from the chill if necessary.

Acclimated to the harsher climate of his homeland, Markus remained unaffected by the dwindling temperatures of summer ushering in fall. The transitioning seasons meant a retreating window for him to return home. If he didn't find the answers the family wanted within three weeks, he'd be stuck in Sziveria until the spring thaw of the Northern Pass.

Rising when the train came to a complete stop, he hefted his pack onto his shoulder. Lunah stepped ahead of him and lead the way off the train. On the sidewalk in front of the station, Markus weighed the benefits of walking to the Sziverian National Investigative Division headquarters, or hiring a carriage. The slow-moving mixture of horse riders, bicyclists, passenger carriages, transportation carts, and the glimpse of an Ariot, a sleek magnetically powered, expensive and therefore rare, single passenger vehicle, made Markus turn right on the sidewalk and push his way through others who opted to walk instead of ride.

Lunah's fur brushed his thigh with each step. He kept his fingers twined in the thick pelt between her shoulders. While she'd never wander, he liked to keep the calm reminder to remain close. A brisk wind blew leaves and common city debris around their feet. Lunah hopped over an empty, cracked glass jar. Her back feet sent it skittering and sliding between the people behind them. The delectable scent of bakery's competed with street vendors cooking meat or frying vegetables. Traffic crawled to a near stop the closer to the government buildings. Tall, boring cement block structures dominated sev eral blocks, their rooftop greenhouses glittering like glass diamonds in the sky.

People entered and exited the SNID building. The warmth of the day failed to penetrate the deep shadows of the recessed doors. Markus waited for an opening in the constant flow of foot traffic to enter. Lunah took the opportunity for them, rushing the door at the first chance. Inside, Lunah sniffed the air, turning to the right when Markus would have gone straight to the stairs Bella preferred to use instead of the main stairway.

This way, her scent is this way, Lunah said.

Markus opened their bond, closing his eyes to better concentrate, and took in the sweet vanilla and berries of Bella lingering in the air among the hundreds of other scent trails. Like threads crossing over each other, all of them went gray while Bella's glowed a vibrant lavender. Sure enough, the thread led to the basement level, not the fifth floor, where she'd worked as a filing clerk for a lead investigative Guardian on the serial crimes team. Markus hesitated.

Why would she be down there?

We won't know unless we go, we won't.

He sighed and pushed the door open to the wide, shadowed downstairs. Hanging lamps barely illuminated the inky depths. Following Lunah, they delved deeper into the underground labyrinth. Markus tried to remember everything Bella had once told him was located in the lowest level. Evidence, which they headed away from. Supply, though he couldn't remember which direction she'd said to go if he ever had a need for paperclips. And long storage, where he wondered if she were located.

Light spilled from a door propped open by a wooden wedge shoved underneath. The whisper of shuffling paper broke the silence. Markus's bag bumped an over stacked shelving unit, causing boxes to rattle. He turned on his heel and held out his hands, making sure nothing fell.

"Intake is on the shelf to your left!" a female voice called. "If anything needs signed for, leave the slip and I'll have it delivered to your floor by the end of the day."

Lunah yipped and spun in an excited circle before taking off in the direction of the voice. A squeal of surprise turned into elated laughter, mingling with Lunah's overjoyed crying.

Happy! My Bella! Lunah chimed through their bond over and over again, making his heart twist.

The unfamiliar sensation of nerves left him motionless. For almost five months he'd been connected to her over letters. The anticipation of seeing her again had ruled his thoughts since learning he'd be returning to Sziveria. Now, with her feet away, he couldn't move. He didn't want to be treated like a stranger, yet what more could he expect? They'd spent a few days together solving a crime, in person they weren't anymore familiar with each other than they'd been in the spring.

Lunah's happy exclamations faded and the rustle of papers sounded. Bella rounded a row of shelves, her dark curls haloed by a lamp behind her. She'd piled the unruly mass onto the top of her head. Most of the strands had escaped at the back and around her temples, leaving her beautiful face framed by whisps. Loose cotton cream pants and a long-sleeved silk navy tunic flowed along her willowy frame. The clothes were more mature than her twenty-three years, and a bit too large for her. And still, she was the most beautiful woman he'd ever seen.

Markus didn't have time to speak. The moment her gaze met his, she broke into a run and launched herself at him. A quick reaction time born from years of training allowed him to catch her instead of being thrown backward by the force of her momentum. Without thought, he picked her up. She wrapped around him, locking her ankles behind his back, her arms squeezing his shoulders. A faint tremble wracked her body as she buried her face in the crook of his neck.

Her embrace held a desperate edge. Markus hugged her tight to his chest. The warmth of her skin clung to the silk beneath his fingers. "What's wrong?" he whispered against her temple.

She shook her head and strengthened her

grip. Lunah sat at his feet, head tilted, a question in her golden eyes.

I don't know what is wrong, Markus said through their bond.

Bella leaned back enough for him to see her remarkable ocean green eyes, startling against her light brown skin. She touched his braid, his neck, the short hair of his beard. Then she shocked him to the center of his being by kissing him.